MARYSUE
RUCCI
BOOKS

ALSO BY HELEN PHILLIPS

HUM

HELEN PHILLIPS

MARYSUE
RUCCI
BOOKS

NEW YORK   LONDON   TORONTO   SYDNEY   NEW DELHI

MARYSUE
RUCCI
BOOKS

Marysue Rucci Books
An Imprint of Simon & Schuster, LLC
1230 Avenue of the Americas
New York, NY 10020

First Marysue Rucci Books hardcover edition August 2024

MARYSUE RUCCI BOOKS and colophon
are trademarks of Simon & Schuster, LLC

Simon & Schuster: Celebrating 100 Years of Publishing in 2024

For information about special discounts for bulk purchases, please contact Simon & Schuster Special Sales at 1-866-506-1949 or business@simonandschuster.com.

The Simon & Schuster Speakers Bureau can bring authors to your live event. For more information or to book an event, contact the Simon & Schuster Speakers Bureau at 1-866-248-3049 or visit our website at www.simonspeakers.com.

Interior design by Laura Levatino

Manufactured in the United States of America

1   3   5   7   9   10   8   6   4   2

Library of Congress Cataloging-in-Publication Data has been applied for.

ISBN 978-1-6680-0883-6
ISBN 978-1-6680-0885-0 (ebook)

This book is for my children,
Ruth & Neal

Poison is in everything, and no thing is without poison.
The dosage makes it either a poison or a remedy.

–PARACELSUS

PART 1

1

The needle inched closer to her eye, and she tried not to flinch.

Above her, the hum hovered, immaculate and precise. The steadiness of metal, the peace of a nonbiological body. She had heard of elderly people who, at the end, chose hum company over human company.

The hum paused to dip its needle-finger in antiseptic yet again, then re-extended its arm, a meticulous surgeon. Its labor was calm, deft, as hum labor always was.

Yet the pain grew crisp as the needle moved across her skin toward the edge of her eye. A slender and relentless line of penetration. The numbing gel must be wearing off.

She had twice endured childbirth by imagining her way out of her body, into a forest, the forest of her childhood, a faint path weaving among evergreens. But now the forest of her childhood was receding even in her memory. She needed to picture some other forest, not that particular forest, which was gone, burned.

A forest. She tried to force her mind into a forest.

The hum retracted the needle and, with the fingers of its other hand, carefully reapplied numbing gel to the area around her eyes.

She felt that the hum had read her mind, though she realized it was simply reacting to the mathematically dictated decrease in the gel's effectiveness over time.

"Please let me know," the hum said, such a soothing voice, "when it is numb again, May."

Long before hums existed, she was one of many hired to help refine and deepen the communicative abilities of artificial intelligence. She had taken satisfaction in the process, in the network's increasing conversational sophistication and nuance, and her small but meaningful role in that progress, until the network exceeded human training and no longer needed their input. But despite all those years of hours spent at her desk, in dialogue with the network, it was very different to be speaking to a hum in person, to have a hum's actual body near her actual body, each of them taking up a similar amount of space in the room. She had never before been this close to a hum for this length of time, for this intimate a procedure. Back when she still had dental insurance, her dentist proudly introduced his new colleague, a hum with dental tools in place of finger attachments. She was tense the whole twenty minutes, her toes clenched inside her shoes, but her teeth had never felt so fresh.

The hum passed her a plastic cup of water. It was not wearied by the hours of labor. Probably there would be someone else after her, another guinea pig, and another, and another, for the hum could go on and on and on, charging remotely, its grace unyielding, while she frayed more by the minute, her body sweating and growing thirsty. The first time she had seen a hum, standing at a bus stop on a sunny day last year, she had mistaken it for a sculpture, clean silver lines of arms and legs and neck linking oblong head and torso and feet, small spheres at elbow and wrist and knee and ankle joints, polished plastic and brushed aluminum, a gleaming thing.

A week later, she saw another hum on the subway, and soon enough, she saw them on a regular basis, dispensing medications at the pharmacy, taking the kids' blood pressure at the pediatrician, patrolling the streets alongside human police officers, in such high demand by government institutions and private corporations that the company who had figured out how to so elegantly embody the expansive brain of the network had a waitlist months long.

"Thank you," she said, accepting the plastic cup of water from the hum.

She sat up in the operating chair to drink the water.

"Do you want to see yourself, May?" the hum said.

"No," she said, "thank you."

She would wait until the end, until the alteration was complete.

Sitting up, momentarily free of the needle, she was overwhelmed by dread.

What if Jem was right.

He had cradled her face in his hands in bed last night, his eyes damp in the lamplight, it had been a long time since he had touched her with such care.

"It's not like I'm going to die," she had said, closing her eyes.

He moved his fingers over her eyelids, her nose and cheeks.

"Money honey," she said, opening her eyes, straining for levity.

"Blood money," he said. "Skin money," he corrected.

"Rent money," she corrected, a flash of rage. "Grocery money. Dental bill money."

He took his hands off her face, turned away from her with a pained sigh, reminding her of other middle-of-the-night conversations that had ended with a pained sigh. Staying up too late, exchanging panic about the children's futures, what will this planet hold for them by the time they're our age.

Deliberately, she placed her hands on top of the knot in her stomach.

In exchange for the use of her face she was being given the equivalent of ten months' worth of her salary at her bread-and-butter job, the solid stabilizing middle-class job that had brought them to the city a decade before, the job that provided certain comforts to which she had become overly, shamefully attached (buying daffodils at the bodega, dropping sixty dollars on dinner out at the diner with the kids for no reason), the job she had lost—because now the network could teach itself, because Nova in HR could only convince May's boss to keep her on for so long once her irrelevance became irrefutable—three months before. As soon as she was released from this room, she would catch up on the overdue rent. And even after she beelined to the ticket booth, did the outrageous thing, the splurge (but it wasn't a splurge, not really—more like a reset button for their entire lives), still there would be a big cushion, eight months maybe, or nine if they could be frugal. She would find another job. Never mind that she hadn't found a job these past three months, the humiliation of her head bobbing on the screen, the unforgiving sheen of her own overhead light on her face, trying to impress someone far away, trying to spin it that it was because she was so excellent at her job that she had lost her job, rendered herself obsolete. She would find another job. Keep the apartment. Have insurance again, or at least be able to pay out of pocket for Lu's dental care, the relentless cavities, and take Sy back to the specialist to help with his fine-motor skills. Buy groceries. Buy the things the kids kept needing: fluoride rinse, rain boots, a birthday gift for a friend. She would take care of it all. And maybe in the meantime Jem would get more gigs. And gigs he liked better. He could do more each day, five or six rather than three or four, if she did mornings and school drop-offs and school pickups and homework and dinner and bedtime with the kids on her own. That would be fine. She could handle that. Maybe he'd get more art-hanging and furniture-arranging than pest disposal. More weird shopping requests than sewage-backup cleanup. You never knew, with the app. Anyway, his ratings were high, unusually high, though he did fret endlessly over the rare negative ones.

This was a solution. So he shouldn't give her a hard time about it. No one should give her a hard time about it. Nova shouldn't give her a hard time about it. Nova shouldn't have texted, seconds after Jem turned away from her with that pained sigh, *Are you sure you're sure about this?*

Though it was Nova who had gotten her going on the whole thing, the two of them grabbing coffee during Nova's lunch break a couple of months after May was fired. The café had screens at every seat, so she had to peer over two screens to see Nova's wide-set eyes, beautiful with kindness, her petite body finally round with eight months of pregnancy after three years of attempted self-insemination and two miscarriages. Nova who, nine years before, upon finding out that May was pregnant with Lu, said, "You have that much hope?" Nova, human resources ambassador, pragmatic and courageous, had withstood all the layoffs at the company. Nova knew someone, a friend of a friend, whose start-up had just gotten funding. "It's a little horrifying though," Nova said. "I shouldn't even tell you about it." But May wanted to be told. Nova ran a finger over the tattoo on her wrist, a subtle geometric design that May had admired from the first moment she met Nova, on the day when Nova processed and fingerprinted her before she started the job, Nova's confident fingers carefully orienting her hand on the screen. The next day, Nova appeared at the door of her tiny office and asked if she wanted to eat lunch together outside, easily generous, *There's a cement slab between this building and the next that gets a crack of sunshine at noon.* Nova had many best friends at work, but May just had Nova. "Adversarial tech," Nova had said in the café, gazing at her over the screens. "You know, like figuring out how to make it so that cams can't recognize you? I kind of love that kind of thing. But still, I don't know if you should do it." This start-up was drowning in money and seeking faces upon which to test their methods.

However, the effect of the procedure—as the vibrant, slightly sexy scientist had promised her over video chat—would be extremely subtle.

This is not radical change. This is barely perceptible change. Certainly not noticeable to acquaintances, and only a bit discernable to your nearest and dearest. Nearest and dearest, he had said that, with pots of cacti and other succulents behind him in a room glowing with windows. Just enough to trick the system, Dr. Haight reassured, just playing a little with the sixty-eight coordinates of your faceprint. Trying out a new nontoxic ink with iridescent pigmentation, not readily visible to the human eye, but tricky for the system. Hard to pin down. Shifts depending on the light in any given space. Your face will become unlearnable. You'll be incognito. Isn't that kind of fun?

Wait, so I'll be untrackable? she'd said.

Well, he said, there's still your gait, etc. And your phone. But say you didn't have your phone on you, then you'd be pretty close to invisible, as far as the system is concerned.

And besides, hadn't she herself—spotting a cam on a lamppost or in a tree, reminded that the air around her was abuzz with data—sometimes had the urge to hide her face or peel it off, to do the same to the faces of her children?

She passed the plastic cup of water back to the hum.

Yeah ok it's so much $$$$, Nova had texted, *but it's your $face$*

I can find more gigs, insomniac Jem had promised insomniac May.

"Is it numb again, May?" the hum inquired, though presumably it already knew that the gel was entering its period of effectiveness.

"It's numb," she said, reclining.

The hum's torso screen had dimmed and muted at some point along the way, but as the hum reached over her to begin the most delicate task of all—the eyelids—the screen brightened and the volume rose, and the breaking news was right in her face: a group of masked people had stormed the offices of a media company, holding their phones out in front of them. Streaming on the screens of the masked people's phones: live feeds of the journalists' children playing at playgrounds, boarding school buses, going to gymnastics class. There was an interview with a hyperventilating journalist who had snuck out via the fire escape, but after fifteen seconds the journalist vanished from the frame; she had to get to her son.

"Your eyes must be dry for this part of the procedure," the hum said, "so I will wait until they are dry, May."

"It's just—" she said.

"I understand, May," the hum said, tilting the smooth oval of its head toward her, the oversized eyes on its face screen gazing at her with what felt like empathy.

The hum switched to a talk show, where the hum who had created the lyrics for the hit pop song "Rake" was being interviewed.

"... accounts for the success of 'Rake' compared to other songs you've generated?" the interviewer was asking the hum.

"Please widen your eyes as much as possible, May," the hum said, readjusting the needle depth.

The diminutive hum height of four-feet-eleven inches seemed particularly diminutive in the large chair across from the interviewer, a broad man with a loud voice.

The hum placed the needle at the corner of her eye.

"Please widen your eyes, May," the hum reminded her.

"... because who needs a soul to compose a soulful song, am I right?" the interviewer said, pleased with his question.

The needle buzzed along her eyelid, a dull hurt that increased by the moment. The numbing gel was already wearing off again, or was perhaps of limited utility when it came to the eyelid itself.

She could hardly bear this tender pain shooting through her, both inside and out, her eyelids and her memories, that overlit office where she had spent so many years of her life, accepting and rejecting different phrases proposed by the network, trying to articulate in simple language why one metaphor worked while another was gibberish, why one expression of sympathy was appropriate while another was offensive.

"...my iteration," the hum on the screen was saying, "my serial number, my specific arrangement of atoms, that has produced the work in question, Dustin. But every creative hum act is predicated on the creative acts of all other—"

The torso screen changed abruptly to a popular show about miniature dogs.

"Hey," she said.

"Yes, May?"

"Go back to that interview." And then, an afterthought: "Please."

But the hum did not go back.

"The interview," she repeated.

Still the hum did not go back.

"Please do not move, May." The hum's tone was as kind as ever. It ran the needle along the lower lid of her right eye. "This requires utmost precision, May."

It was common knowledge that hums were designed to obey human requests. To do no harm to humans. Yet this not-small, dexterous hum who had just defied her instruction was manipulating a needle within a millimeter of her eyeball.

She held her breath.

After a moment, the hum lifted the needle.

"That interview was causing you to become tense, May," the hum said. "So I had to change it. You seem to be in pain, May."

At first she heard this as a judgment about her emotional state, but then the hum reached over to apply more of the numbing gel.

"Please return to the interview," she said.

The hum manifested the interview. The interviewer was reaching his large hand out to shake the hum's slim hand.

"It's over," she said, disappointed.

The hum muted and dimmed the torso screen. Her words—*It's over*—endured in the room for many minutes, their spell unbroken by any new conversation.

The numbing gel worked its magic, and she sacrificed herself to the hum's methodical ministrations, half dozing under the needle for some period of time. Her daze was interrupted by the ding of her phone, in her bag on the hook by the door.

Jem, surely, asking how everything had gone.

Knowing that his text awaited her made her newly impatient with the procedure. She wanted to be out of this chair, reunited with her phone, with all the notifications she had missed these past couple of hours. And she had to get to the ticket booth before it closed. Her dozy state receded, replaced by restlessness.

"Are you almost done?" she said to the hum.

"We are almost done, May," the hum replied.

She could request therapy mode. Nova had tried hum therapy before and claimed to get something out of it. Said it wasn't so different from therapy with a human. A little strange, at first, but once you got used to it, there was that same feeling of being listened to. And, cheaper. May, though, had no idea how she'd reply to the standard starter questions at this particular moment: *What are you feeling? Where do you feel it in your body?*

She could request music. But the thought of choosing a type of music, much less an artist, overwhelmed her.

Birdsong, she thought, a lightbulb.

"Could you live stream birdsong?" she said.

"Tropical or forest, May?" the hum said.

She thought of the forest of her childhood. And of her parents, installed—after the fires, the scant insurance payments—in a sedate condominium on a perfectly paved cul-de-sac in a suburban subdivision thirty miles away from the burned forest, where they now tried to live an extraordinarily quiet life, apart from the world, off the internet, spending more than they should on birdseed in an attempt to lure birds to their small deck.

"Forest," she said. Those paths she had walked daily from the time she could walk until she was eighteen years old. She hadn't known the last time was the last time. "Rocky Mountains."

The room filled with birdsong that was traveling, instant by instant, almost two thousand miles to arrive at her ear canals. The birdsong had a physiological effect on her, aching delight, her eardrums straining to hear all the layers.

"The number of birds in the northern part of the continent has declined by three billion, or twenty-nine percent, over the past fifty years, May," the hum said.

"Stop," she said.

"My apologies, May. This live stream is sponsored by the Society for the Preservation of Wildlife."

The needle continued its journey around her left eye. The birds continued to sing. As the numbing gel wore off, she became acutely aware of the bright line of sheer pain moving slowly across her eyelid. For once, the hum did not seem attuned to her discomfort.

She was about to say something when the hum withdrew the needle and spoke: "We are done, May."

The hum hinged forward at the hips so she could look up at her face on the torso screen.

It took a jolt of courage, hands in fists, for her to meet her own gaze.

Did she look different? Or did she only look different because she was expecting to look different?

The differences were subtle, even more subtle than she had antici-pated, and her first reaction was relief—just faint shifts in shading, mi-nuscule alterations to the known topography, her features wavering a bit between familiarity and unfamiliarity, the way she might look in a pic-ture taken from a strange angle.

Entranced, she stared at herself, trying to understand her face. She couldn't put her finger on what had changed in these intervening hours. All the minute deviations added up to some sort of transformation, un-deniable but also undetectable.

What would Jem say.

"Beautiful, May," the hum said. She sensed that the hum was not de-claring her beautiful but rather was reacting to its own handiwork. "This will present an interesting challenge for the system."

Her face felt sore, as though badly sunburned.

"It will feel raw for a few days, May," the hum said. It placed its metal digits on her forehead, the coolness a balm.

Then the hum opened a drawer at the base of the operating chair and withdrew a gauzy gray scarf.

"Allow me, May," the hum said, gingerly wrapping the fabric around the lower half of her face. "This will protect you while you heal. Certain facial expressions may strain you for a week or so. I input two prescrip-tions for you at the pharmacy down the street, an oral pain medication as well as a topical antibacterial cream. Do you want them delivered to your home today?"

"I'll just pick them up."

"I can arrange for them to be delivered to your home, May."

"I can pick them up." She wondered how much they would cost. She had lost her prescription insurance when she lost her job. "And, the—compensation?"

"Was direct-deposited into your account three minutes ago, May."

She got up off the operating chair. Her legs, she discovered, unsteady.

"There is another rejuvenating face crème that might be of help to you. Rosehip and cucumber. Would you like me to order it for you now, May?"

"You mean another prescription?"

"Not exactly," the hum said, "but it does have anti-aging properties. Do you approve this transaction, May?"

She kicked herself for not noticing when the hum switched into advertising. She had felt, after being enwrapped in the hum's attentive care for these hours, after the odder moments in their conversation, a certain affinity with this hum.

"No," she said.

"Did you know that people can tell how old a woman is by the way her hands look, even if she is otherwise well-preserved?" the hum said. "Could I interest you in a hand lotion tailored to your age group, May?"

"No," she said, though her hands had in fact been chapped lately. Though the hum, denied, took on a slight wounded quality. She stepped toward the hook, removed her bag. "No thank you."

"Those jeans would look better with slouchy boots, May," the hum said.

She was still saying "No thank you" as she exited into the hallway, the metal door closing behind her, the hum offering her something else. She dug around in her bag for her phone, and couldn't find it, and kept digging. When at last her fingers located it, she seized it, desperate to read Jem's text.

You've been selected to try our new Premier Surprise Sweets service!

2

She stood on the sidewalk outside the medical complex and tapped the link in the overdue rent warning email. Another tap, and another, and rent plus interest, paid. Then, another tap to submit the grocery order she had prepared the day before. The food would reach their home before dinner. She smiled. The smile strained her skin.

She began a text to Jem, wishing he had written to her.

I don't feel disfigured, she wrote.

She deleted the words.

Paid! she wrote instead, and sent it.

Her prescriptions, her phone informed her, were ready for pickup. The pharmacy in question was a block and a half away. She could spy its red-and-blue sign from here.

She dropped her phone into her bag and began to walk. The smell of exhaust. The colorless buildings of a piece with the colorless pavement of a piece with the colorless sky. Even the trees in their squares of dirt, even the blowing bits of litter, were drained of color.

Crossing the single street that lay between her and the pharmacy, she glanced up and saw, above the walk signal, a cam.

A fist-punch of a laugh shot out of her.

Inside the store, she hurried to the pharmacy counter in the back, hungry for relief. The pharmacy was empty aside from an elderly man requesting a litany of prescriptions, some of which weren't yet approved for refill, as a hum was politely trying to explain over the old man's high-pitched declarations that of course they were approved for refill, he had been taking them for years.

As she waited, she heard familiar chords coming through a speaker mounted on the ceiling. A favorite song of hers from when she was a teenager, just a guitar and a voice, a melody at once catchy and tender, a goodbye song. The volume was low, and she strained to catch a lyric or two, the particular magic it held for her diluted by the fluorescence of the pharmacy.

"I understand your frustration," the hum said, "and I am confident that I can help you resolve these issues, Matthew."

"I need a person," Matthew said.

Her face throbbed. She turned to stroll down the nearest aisle—makeup—while they sorted it out. Speed-walking down the aisle toward the pharmacy counter came a human employee, "FREY," looking at once weary and overzealous.

"Your prescriptions aren't approved for refill yet," Frey explained brightly.

"Yeah yeah yeah yeah yeah," Matthew said.

Makeup. Not that she'd dare put anything on her face anytime soon. Halfway down the aisle, she came to a display of beeswax lip balms. Cardamom, lavender, eucalyptus, lemon rind, bergamot. Expensive, though. Extravagant. She ran her fingers over the bamboo tubes. But she had already selected her indulgence for the day. For the month, the year. She listened to the distorted croon of the song she once loved, sitting on a park bench splitting earbuds with someone, underage with vodka in a plastic water bottle.

She turned the corner, into the aisle of school supplies. So many things it would be fun to give them. Things that would make them happy. A pack of six rolls of polka-dot tape for Sy. Forty-eight colored pencils for Lu. Rhinestone stickers. Metallic markers. Glitter glue. She shouldn't linger.

Matthew and Frey were gone when she returned to the pharmacy counter. The hum scanned her face.

The scan failed, a red error screen flashing before her.

Though of course she knew the scan would fail, was supposed to fail, still it jarred her, a jolt of panic through her body.

"Can you please fully remove your face covering and I will try again?" the hum said, unable to personalize the question with her name.

"Let's just do fingerprint," she said, forcing nonchalance into her voice.

The hum manifested the fingerprint option, and she lined her hand up with the silhouette of the hand on the torso screen. It always felt like a slight violation, undeservedly intimate, to touch a hum there, even though she had done it plenty of times. To order a drink at a noisy bar. To verify the kids at the pediatrician.

The torso glowed green with recognition.

"Two prescriptions are ready for you," the hum said. "Do you approve this transaction, May Webb?"

"I approve." For the first time in three months, her stomach didn't tighten as she said those words.

"Your prescriptions are arriving, May," the hum said. Two bags glided down the conveyer belt toward her. "Did you know that people can tell how old a woman is by the way her hands look, even if she is otherwise well-preserved? Could I interest you in a hand lotion tailored to your age group, May?"

"No thank you."

"Did you know that we offer beeswax lip balm in five all-natural flavors, May?"

She turned away from the counter—*no thank you no thank you*—and walked down the drinks aisle, the refrigerated buzz. A craving overtook her. Not a craving for anything in particular; just the realization that she wanted to buy something to drink, to consume. She considered many different colorful options, unable to settle on anything.

Her phone dinged, and she grabbed it, wondering what he'd written back to her. *How excited are you for your new Premier Surprise Sweets service!?!*

She opened the glass door and pulled out a wild cherry seltzer. She and Jem used to buy wild cherry seltzers on Sunday afternoons in the summertime, back before the kids were born. They'd put the seltzers in the freezer for half an hour. Lie on the floor of their scarcely furnished apartment in the overwhelming heat. A droplet of cold seltzer in her belly button.

Her pain swelled, demanded attention. She paid for the seltzer with her fingerprint at the self-service checkout by the exit and rushed outside. Immediately she missed the air-conditioning. She stood in front of the store, struggling to penetrate the layers of packaging encasing the topical cream: the staples, the paper bag, the plastic bag, the plastic wrapping, the box, the tape, the puncture top. Finally there was a caterpillar of lotion on her index finger. She spread it along her forehead, her cheeks, beneath her eyes, the drug disseminating a numbing calm across her skin. Then she extricated a pain pill from the other pharmacy bag.

She twisted the top off the wild cherry seltzer, pain pill dissolving into the fizz of seltzer in her mouth. How good things felt, sometimes: the cream on her face, the sizzle in her throat.

She drank deep of the seltzer before noticing a clear sticker on the bottle. It blended so well into the label that she could not tell whether it was part of the packaging or sabotage of the packaging: *Five hundred million plastic bottles are discarded in your city each year!* read the crimson lettering.

She dropped the plastic bottle to the bottom of her bag.

3

The subway was six blocks away. The booth for discounted last-minute tickets was three stops away on the subway. The booth would close in less than forty-five minutes. She could vee. She could afford to vee, now. But given the amount of money she was about to spend, she should probably take the train.

Waiting to cross the street, she watched a pigeon land on the roof of a van stopped at the light. The bird stood on the van, serene. When the light changed and the van moved, the bird panicked and flapped, shocked.

There was a donut shop by the entrance to the subway station. In the dull cast of the day, the donuts in the window glowed. She paused, noticed her hunger. To think that humans, once prey in the wild, had arrived at this. These glazes and sprinkles.

The reflection of her face.

The door of the shop was propped open to the bland, humid day. A barista called out, "Bagel with butter?" And then, a moment later, plaintively, "Bagel with butter?"

As she stepped across the threshold, her phone dinged. Jem.

Air Quality Warning issued in your area from now until 10 p.m.

The donuts in the window, she realized, were fakes; the real donuts were stored in metal bins behind the counter.

She was wasting her time. She hurried out of the donut shop without buying anything, half ran to the subway entrance and descended the stairs.

Passing through the turnstile she spotted a cam, its single attentive eye trained down on her face, and something flickered within her, a lightness, a light-headedness.

The train would come in three minutes. She couldn't hold still. Her body quivering. She paced the platform, giddy, ghostly, her feet not quite solid on the concrete.

A moist, unclean wind heralded the train's arrival. She looped the gauze scarf around to protect more of her face.

On the screens in the train, an ad for a sixty-four-date hologram tour with a popular singer who had been dead for twenty-seven years.

A woman in New Zealand had been arrested for going into grocery stores and hiding needles inside strawberries.

A music video of a teenager with gray hair against a gray background, pulling at their face with jerky motions.

A pair of high school girls in Florence, Italy, had been caught on cam stealing all the good-luck coins tossed into a sixteenth-century fountain, vandalizing with golden spray paint the sculpture of Bacchus, taking off their clothes, kissing in the water. There was footage, mesmerizing footage, largely obscured by night—their naked backs, the splashing water, the paint glistening on the marble. Additional cams had identified them hours later, entering a Catholic school in uniform.

According to a new survey, more humans had experienced intense negative emotions in the past calendar year than at any other time in recorded history.

May forced her attention away from the screens. Most of the people in the car—an old woman with a bag of clementines on her lap, a young man with a violin case, a trio of teenagers, a toddler in a stroller—were earbudded and absorbed in phones. A hum stood at rest in the middle of the car, requiring neither seat nor pole, perfectly balanced on its oblong feet, meditative in appearance.

Strange, that now no stranger could snap a picture of her with their phone and immediately know most everything about her.

The train creaked out of the underground tunnel onto the above-ground bridge, pale light filling the car. It was childish to stand up and go to the twin windows of the sliding doors to get a better view, but she did it anyway. From here she could see blocks of graffitied rooftops and water towers and solar panels. A new condominium building with concrete stilts elevating it above the flood line. A balcony turned into a miniature forest with potted plants. A tiny old graveyard, green pocked with gray. Far away, the harbor, a rusted cargo ship. In an abandoned lot alongside the unnaturally turquoise canal, a shelter made of orange and brown tarps. And, in the distance, the vast walls of the Botanical Garden.

Her phone dinged in her bag.

That's good you okay love?

Jem, at last. She was glad.

But were the words his own, or were they an option offered him by his phone? He never called her "love" and was generally meticulous with commas and periods. Then again, he could have been in a rush, which would explain the poor punctuation and the uncharacteristic term of endearment, shorthand for tenderness he didn't have time to express. But Jem's phone knew that the occasional dropped piece of punctuation was typical of his texting tendencies at times, the error evidence of authenticity, and so the phone might reproduce the error, in order to reproduce the authenticity.

Her phone suggested three potential responses to Jem's text: *Yes!* or *Doing great!* or *All good.*

It hurts, she wrote, and then added, *but I'm happy*.

Good, Jem replied, so instantaneously that there was only one explanation.

She dropped her phone into her bag. The train rattled back underground. Her stop was next. The gauze scarf felt harsh on her skin. She loosened it.

Her phone dinged, and she reached for it, curious to see what he had written to complicate his pre-made response.

Click here to accept your new Premier Surprise Sweets service!!

When she looked up from her phone, the toddler in the stroller was staring at her. She drew the gauze scarf across her face as she stepped off the train.

4

The ticket booth was on an inconspicuous street, nothing to mark it as the pathway to other vistas. Clumps of damp litter, discarded cigarette butts. Now whenever she saw a cigarette butt she thought of that tantrum Sy threw a few months back when he wanted to put a cigarette butt he harvested from the sidewalk into the dollhouse to serve as a paper-towel roll.

The line stretched a quarter of the way down the block. She wasn't alone in seeking the five-percent eleventh-hour in-person discount.

She took her place at the end of the line. The heat of the day had a weight to it, an odor. A slight sting in her eyes from poor air quailty. The woman in front of her was pregnant, beads of sweat at her temples. She smiled at the woman. The smile the woman returned to her was limp, as though her face wasn't accustomed to forming such an expression. The woman shifted her weight away from May and dove into her phone.

The line inched forward.

She wished she had been able to go to the Botanical Garden when she was pregnant.

The pregnant woman raised her eyes from her phone, shot May a don't-look-at-me look. She hadn't realized she was staring. Embarrassed, she focused her gaze on the screen mounted above the ticket booth, which was playing the promo for the Botanical Garden on a loop. She had watched it countless times before, but she never tired of it. The close-ups of ferns and flowers. The stone bridge over the brook. The tree sagging with fruit. The waterfall, white spray on green rocks. The bedrooms, their little jars of lavender, their wooden furniture and blue bedspreads. A handful of birds taking flight from a lilac bush.

And that promo could be infinitely augmented by her phone, by the effervescent social media posts of the guests. She likes she likes she likes she likes she likes, but in truth she could hardly stand to look at them at all. On any other day, she wouldn't torture herself by seeking out such images. These selfies and just-a-little-moment-of-bliss shots gushing forth from those vacationing at the Botanical Garden, jam-packed with flora, fauna, plates of richly colored food, earthenware mugs filled to the brim, wooden boxes of truffles, hands overflowing with berries, feet wading into clean water, children running through meadows, human faces in various states of relaxation, a resplendent hum bearing a bowl of peaches.

"Next guest, please," said the hum inside the ticket booth, its voice a notch louder than normal, its eyes on the friendliest setting.

She pulled herself out of her phone and realized that the hum had already addressed her more than once.

Her legs were unsteady as she stepped up to the window, as the facial scan failed (surge of fear, guilt), as she requested fingerprint and placed her hand on the hum's torso, green light of recognition.

"Hello, May Webb," the hum said.

She found herself short of breath.

Jem would be so upset. Worried about money. The kids would be ecstatic.

"How many visitors, May?"

"Four."

"Any children, May?"

"Two."

"Ages, May?"

"Eight and six."

"Full names, May?"

"Lu Webb-Clarke and Sy Webb-Clarke."

"And the other adult, May?"

"Jem Clarke."

"How many nights, May?"

Two, or three? Three, or two? She hadn't yet decided, had been rolling the question around in her mind for days. Two meant Jem would be slightly less distressed. Three meant more joy. Three meant her profligacy was undeniable.

"Three, please," she said.

"Basic or Deluxe, May?"

"Basic, please."

"You are a lucky person, May," the hum said. "We just had a cancellation for a three-night Basic for two adults and two children. Entry is tomorrow at the west gate at seven thirty a.m. Do you approve this transaction, May?"

Still short of breath.

"Do you approve this transaction, May?" the hum repeated, after waiting the proper interval.

"I approve," she said, and the money vanished from the account.

"Congratulations, May," the hum said.

She smiled, wildly.

"We recommend that you purchase one of our Traveler Paks, May. The Essential Traveler Pak includes sunscreen, insect repellent, tweezers, alcohol swabs, two matching bandanas, two flashlights, a packet of Band-Aids, and a stainless-steel water bottle."

"Yes," she said, "I want that."

"However, in your case, considering the children, I highly recommend an upgrade to the Enhanced Traveler Pak, May. With the Enhanced, you will find that the sunscreen and the insect repellent are organic, and it includes spare batteries, as well as four matching bandanas and four—"

"The Essential is fine," she said.

"Do you approve this transaction, May?"

"I approve." She didn't even have to think about the money if she didn't want to. It was taken from her so silently, so swiftly.

"The Essential Traveler Pak is en route to your home, May. May you have the time of your life."

5

May. May you have the time of your life.

The sound of the receipt pinging into her phone. She soared away from the ticket booth, back toward the subway, her body jittery with the beautiful choices she had made.

She was halfway down the block when her skin demanded her attention. Eyes watering, face an ache. She needed to apply another layer of cream.

Her ecstasy, her extravagance, intermingled with her pain, with her need for a private place, and suddenly she was summoning a vee, and ninety seconds later an empty silver car pulled up in front of her.

When the vee failed to recognize her face—error message on the screen above the door handle—she unlocked the door with her fingerprint. She could have chosen any of the five seats, but habit found her buckling up in the back seat.

"Good afternoon, May Webb," the vee said.

"Hi," she said, grabbing around in her bag for the tube of cream, her need for it intensifying by the second.

At last she found it, smeared it across her face, shut her eyes, glad to be alone. She waited for the numbness to set in.

"Is seventy-three degrees Fahrenheit good for you, May?" the vee said.

"That's perfect, thanks."

She smiled, soothed, that feeling of being taken care of, a break from the heat and the exhaust, the dark upholstery suffused with the fragrance of cedar, the lovely glide. She would have kept her eyes shut but there was, playing on the large screen at the front of the vee, an ad for a drive-in vegan restaurant. One block later, they passed the drive-in vegan restaurant.

"Could you turn off the screen, please?" she said.

Once the screen was off, once the vee fell silent, then she would be at peace.

"I can turn it off, May," the vee said, "for a three-percent ad-free surcharge."

Animals paying machines for tranquility. She wanted to laugh about it with Jem. That was all she really wanted, ever.

"Never mind," she said to the vee.

There was an ad for a dinner delivery service for tired parents. She noted the name of the service.

She got a text from the vee app, asking her to rate her vee experience.

She watched her progress on the map, the small lime-green dot of herself.

She tried to remember the name of the dinner delivery service, but already it had slipped her mind.

She wondered if he would text her again.

She typed into her phone "hiking shoes for Bo" and the auto-text took over: "tanical Garden."

Something landed against the windshield with a hard and horrifying thud, and the vee torqued to the right. Or did the vee torque and then the hard and horrifying thud?

Her breath was ripped from her body, but when finally she was able to bring some air back into herself, she heard herself crying out. By then the vee had come to a standstill at an awkward angle, the right front wheel up on the curb.

Out the window, there was a body on the pavement in the crosswalk.

It was a hum, so no blood.

But a body on the pavement looks like a body on the pavement.

Not a body, she told herself, not a body.

If she had not been making this particular journey on this particular day at this particular time, that figure would still be upright.

That exploded arm, metal and plastic scattered across the street.

"Why did you hit it?" she said to the vee accusingly, trembling.

"A delivery vehicle ran the red light. I swerved in order to protect you, May."

Vanishing down the street, the unmistakable pink, the unmistakable logo, on the back of one of the ever-present delivery vans for the everything store.

The vee backed up off the curb, restored its proper positioning on the street.

She looked again at the fallen hum in the crosswalk and was surprised to see two hums standing over it. Where had they come from? Then another hum joined them, and a fourth. With infinite gentleness, the hums knelt down as one, lifted the wounded hum, carried it to the sidewalk. A fifth hum appeared and began gathering up the hum parts scattered in the crosswalk.

On the screen at the front of the vee: *Did you know that people can tell how old a woman is by the way her hands look, even if she is otherwise well-preserved?*

Her vee pulled away, continued onward. In the rearview mirror, a hum repair vehicle arrived without fanfare. Aside from the lack of red and blue lights, it looked like an ambulance. The hums surrounded the fallen hum, their bodies protective and reverent as they prepared it for transfer to the repair vehicle. Something strange in her, a flash of envy?

There are new chewable daily vitamins crafted especially for women like you to promote healing from within.

She was still trembling. She stared out the window. She would be home in less than ten minutes. She had dazzling news for them and a face that was almost identical to the face they knew.

On the screen, ads chattered and sang.

"Have a spectacular day, May," the vee said, pulling up in front of her building, opening its door for her, a text arriving to request that she rate her ride.

"You have a spectacular day too," she said automatically, inanely.

She stepped out of the vee and bequeathed it five stars.

Their building was timeworn and untended, with a front door that still required a physical key. She stood on the sidewalk fumbling for her key chain. When she entered the lobby, she saw stacked there four pink boxes with the familiar logo, the same logo adorning the delivery van that had decimated the hum in the crosswalk.

Each of the packages bore her name.

6

It was an unwieldy load, especially with the interference of the gauze scarf, but somehow she managed to pile all four boxes in her arms. She placed her raw chin gingerly atop the smallest box and made her way toward the stairs. Her face wasn't as numb as she wanted it to be. She was halfway up the first flight when her phone dinged in her bag. She should wait until she was home, but she couldn't wait. She used her knee to prop the boxes against the peeling paint of the brick wall, freeing her right hand to search for and scoop out her phone.

All okay?

She had only one hand available and four boxes weighing her down, and her face hurt and the hum was destroyed, and she was suspicious of that *All okay?*, doubtful Jem had selected those words himself, and so, with the wispiest touch of her pinky, she sacrificed herself to one of the ready-made replies:

All good!

A prickle of regret. That artificial exclamation mark.

Less than a second after she dropped her phone into the depths of her bag, it dinged again; again, the search and scoop.

What will your first Surprise Sweet be!?

She arrived finally at the fifth floor and put the boxes down and extricated her keys from her bag. The door opened into that particular silence that could mean only one thing. She didn't even need to check the heart app to know. With her feet she pushed the boxes into the uncanny quiet of the apartment.

She locked the door behind her. She used her right foot to remove her left shoe and her left foot to remove her right shoe. She lined the shoes up by the door. She lined the boxes up on the kitchen counter.

She shouldn't turn on the air conditioner, the money, the waste. It wouldn't take long to adapt to the airlessness of the small apartment. Tomorrow, she would be in the woods.

But she couldn't resist pressing the button and standing before the machine, enveloped in a breeze so cool she had the sensation of mint on her tongue. She would turn it off soon. Pretty soon.

There was so much to do that for a long while she couldn't do any of it. It was better to stay right here with the air conditioner numbing her face.

Out the window, the air looked hazy. Smoke blowing in from distant fires.

She looked at her phone to check the air quality but, before she could tap the AQI icon, an ad for donuts filled the screen, a slow pan across an array of glazed and besprinkled donuts like those she had longed for in the shopwindow.

She skipped the ad. Another—for hiking shoes—took its place, continuing to obscure the air quality icon. The phone made it easy to order four pairs. The phone knew the correct size for each person in the family. Just as the phone had known, on that winter day more than eight years ago, before she realized it herself, *YOU ARE PREGNANT!*

She selected six-hour express delivery, trying not to think about the delivery van and the hum in the crosswalk, and then pulled out a knife to open the largest box, a shudder of self-disgust as knife sliced tape.

She opened the flaps of the box, an ashamed rather than exuberant Christmas, a mess of Styrofoam packing peanuts: What had she ordered this time? A pair of colorful cloth pieces? She had no memory of purchasing such things. A packet of alcohol swabs? There was some mix-up. She hadn't bought this random junk. Only when she gripped a pair of tweezers did she realize. The Essential Traveler Pak.

She turned her attention to the smallest box. She had no idea what was in this one, either, until she penetrated the tape and remembered: a bottle of evergreen room spray. She could already picture Jem rolling his eyes. Can you please stop spending money like someone who still has a middle-class salary. Forty-six orders in the past three months. But she wanted to envelop her children in the scent of trees. She knifed through the plastic wrapping and spritzed the kitchen with the fragrance. The scent was not as crisp as she craved.

The third box contained groceries, the order she had placed after the procedure, a salad in a plastic shell, a log of mozzarella, stuff for the kids' lunches. Applesauce pouches, individual yogurt cups, string cheese, apples from Argentina.

By the time she got to the fourth box, the counter was covered with packaging detritus, Bubble Wrap and Styrofoam and plastic. She opened the box with trepidation. Inside she discovered a roll of dental floss, a roll of double-sided tape, a roll of toilet paper, an outlet splitter, and a slim metal ruler. Typical random Jem order.

They needed to stop spending money.

She put the tape and the outlet splitter and the ruler on Jem's chaotic little desk crammed in the corner of the single room that served as living and dining room. Put the toilet paper under the bathroom sink and the dental floss in the mirrored cabinet, already picturing the day when the dental floss would be used up, its plastic container empty.

Her hands smelled like plastic so she washed them.

Standing there with the water running over her hands, she closed her eyes and breathed, the first time she had been aware of her own breathing in days.

She saw a forest growing, trees maturing and then harvested and pulped and transformed into toilet paper.

She thought of the grand total of all the heartbeats produced by everyone on the planet each day.

She thought of the quantity of toilet paper required.

The apartment smelled vaguely of garbage. Six roses—which she had bought for herself on the day she decided to sell her face—were beginning to rot in their glass vase on the table, petals marooning at the edges, stems turning the water gray.

She gripped the roses and pulled them, dripping and stinking, out of the vase. She rushed them to the kitchen trash can. Then she fetched the bathroom trash to consolidate it with the kitchen trash before bagging it all up. The tampons and the roses together, the blood and the flowers, multiple reds against the plastic. She tied the garbage bag and took it out to the landing.

She came back inside and locked the door behind her and committed to being energetic. She turned off the air conditioner and got a few things out of the fridge, the salad shell, the mozzarella, a bag of baby carrots.

But her hands were quivering. She faltered. Craved her woom.

The truth was that when she had glimpsed her face—different, slightly—in the bathroom mirror, it had unsettled her.

If it unsettled her, what would it do to them.

She tugged her old yoga mat out of the back of the coat closet and unrolled it on the kitchen floor. It had been a long time since she'd used it. She sat on the mat on her knees but she couldn't remember what to do next. She knew she was supposed to breathe. She knew she was supposed to say *om*. Outside, the wail of a siren started up, moving ever closer. She knew she was supposed to integrate the interference.

She stood up and rolled the yoga mat and returned it to its banishment in the closet. She opened the cupboard, grateful that she didn't have to take such careful stock of its contents anymore. She grabbed a box of spaghetti and filled the big pot with water and turned on the burner.

She pulled out her phone and tapped the heart app, just to confirm. The four small hearts—so often spread out at school, at work, in the streets, on the subway, beating in different places at the same pace—overlapped on her screen, piled on top of each other, joined at this single address, in this single apartment, merged into one large swelling heart.

7

It was Sy's footsteps she heard first, coming out of the children's room and down the hallway, his unmistakable lightness, paired with the unsteady gait of someone who has just spent a spell of time inside a woom.

"Hey," she said, pausing in her task of sorting the carrots, removing the slimy ones.

She loved to look at him.

"I'm a baby cockroach," he said, gazing at the floor. "I'm delicate and I die easily."

She stepped away from the counter and picked him up, her arms a hammock. He was almost too big to be held this way. But she summoned her strength and he leaned back, eyes closed.

Some weeks ago, the children had slipped into May and Jem's room in the middle of the night, Sy's hands sheltering the cockroach Lu bore on her palm. *Where did you find that?* Jem said. *I can't remember*, Lu said. *My bed*, Sy said. *She's an orphan*, Lu said, *she has no family, she wants to be part of our family.* Sy said, *Do you think she'd like to watch* Swan & Hen *with us? Look at her cutie face. What should we name her?* When they finally got the kids settled back down to sleep, the cockroach—"Coco"—

in a jam jar on the kitchen counter, May and Jem argued about whether to keep it or kill it, switching sides moment by moment, but Coco didn't make it through the night, probably already woozy from the exterminator's poison by the time the children found it. The next afternoon, they received a note from Lu's teacher, offering condolences; she had heard from Lu that their pet had died.

"Heavy guy," she said now to the baby cockroach, preparing to release him.

He opened his eyes, then screamed and wriggled out of her arms and ran to the couch and buried himself in the cushions.

Her face.

Quick, unsteady footsteps came down the hall: Lu, anxious, yanked from her woom by Sy's scream. "What's wrong with him?"

Before May could reply, Lu froze and stared at her mother's face.

"Is it that bad?" May said, her body hot with panic.

Lu hesitated, fingering the blue bunny on her wrist.

"It's not bad," she said at last. "It's just weird."

"I didn't know you were home," Jem said, emerging from the bedroom, his voice lethargic from his time in his woom. "Let's see."

May rotated toward him.

He looked at her.

Dizziness overwhelmed her.

She had made a mistake, an obscene mistake.

"It's okay," Jem said, cautiously.

May glanced at the couch, where Sy was still hiding his face.

"It's really okay," Jem assured. "I just have a slightly new wife."

"Maybe we could get used to it after a while," Lu said.

"But it's not actually that dramatic," May said, "right?"

"Yes," Lu agreed. "That's what's creepy about it. Did it hurt?"

"It was worth it, I think."

"Worth it?" Lu said.

"Worth it"—she paused, trying to summon the giddiness she had imagined she would feel when she told them—"for four three-night passes to the Botanical Garden."

"Wait, what?" Jem said.

"What—what—really, the Botanical Garden?" Lu said.

Sy sprang up from the couch, jumped into the air, "Botanical Garden!" landed with a thud.

Lu began to cry.

"Penelope says there are strawberries that grow out of the ground," Lu said. "She says they give you soft chocolates dusted with chocolate powder. She says there are deer and rabbits and chipmunks."

"Which can gather up to 165 acorns a day," Sy said.

Jem sank down onto the couch. She felt his eyes on her.

"We need every penny," he said.

"Look at them," she said.

The children were levitating around the living room, leaping from couch to coffee table to chair to floor and back again.

"You should have—" he said.

"Your daughter is crying for joy," she interrupted, but the worry on his face weakened her, the adrenaline of the day draining away from her.

She sank down onto the couch beside him. Their thighs touching, the familiar warmth. His hand accepted hers, but he didn't match her squeeze.

"There's still a lot of money left," she said.

Her own money, earned with her very own defaced face.

"It's an unforgettable experience," she said, borrowing language from the online brochure, but he was making her doubt herself. "I mean, don't you want to go?"

"Of course I do, who doesn't," he said. "But in a few months we'll be longing for that extra money. You know we will."

"There's still a lot of money," she repeated, even though he was right. "It'll get us through until I get a job."

"What job?" he said.

She couldn't stand the despair in his voice, the twin of her own despair. Her job had been their sustenance, his gig work keeping them out of the red while he waited for the world to need a professional photographer. Now, working double time, he couldn't keep them afloat.

"I saw something about the museum hiring people to go into schools and pretend to be from the olden days," she said. "Like, doing presentations about how landlines and CDs worked."

"That's a gig," he said.

"Listen," she said, "we'll do this one special thing." Her voice sounded thin, childlike, to her own ears. "And then I'll figure everything out." After the Botanical Garden, she'd reformat her résumé, call her mother, text her cousin, impress interviewers, encourage Jem to pull out his old camera, bake a loaf of banana bread for Nova, go over to meet the baby. "We need to be at the west gate at seven thirty tomorrow morning."

"Tomorrow?" he said with alarm.

"No school?" Lu wept, grinning.

"No first grade!" Sy singsonged, dancing among them, making sharp movements with his elbows, his green bunny waggling wildly on his wrist.

"Block out the next four days in the app," she told Jem. "Skip a few gigs."

"My regulars will wonder where I am," he said. "I'm supposed to check mousetraps tomorrow, and clean out a fridge filled with rotting food, and get all the glitter up off someone's kid's floor, and deliver a dead pet to the taxidermist."

"Can't you release those gigs and someone else will take them?"

It struck her that the pasta water had been boiling, unheeded, for many minutes. She ran to pour the pasta in. Jem followed her.

"We can do other nice things," he said. "We can take the subway out to the beach any weekend. That's worked fine for us for years."

It was hard, though, keeping the kids out of the oily water, look don't touch.

If only the forests hadn't burned. If only the cul-de-sac where her parents lived didn't require plane travel or renting a car and driving for days. If only his parents weren't in Canada. If only it wasn't so hard, so expensive, getting out of the city, getting beyond the many rings of industry and blight, getting to some semblance of nature.

"Can't you return the tickets?" he said.

"No refunds or returns," she lied. "I got the five-percent eleventh-hour discount."

"Fuck," he whispered, but not angrily, just with fatigue. "Then I guess we have to have fun."

She stopped stirring the pasta and looked over at him, unsure about his tone. He gave her that wry smile of his, and she smiled back, straining her face.

"Kids!" Jem said. "The Longs are going to think their ceiling is caving in."

May returned to sorting out the slimy carrots while Jem wrangled the kids into sitting down at the table to submit their homework.

"Is a banana alive?" Sy said, staring at his bunny.

"But aren't we not even going to school tomorrow?" Lu said.

"You still need to submit your homework," Jem said.

"Is a banana alive?" Sy repeated.

May went over and peered at the small screen of his bunny. He had to sort things into two categories: *Living* or *Nonliving*. The screen bore a half-eaten banana.

"I guess a banana is alive," she said.

"Gross, then we're eating live bananas," Lu said from across the table where she was scrolling on her bunny.

"Or maybe by the time you're eating the banana, it's nonliving," May said uncertainly.

"Gross, then we're eating dead bananas," Lu said.

"I hate this assignment," Sy said.

"Who's not mature," Lu said.

"I hate you," Sy said.

"Stop," May said, without muscle.

"According to the article, how many pieces of plastic did Dr. Pierre find inside the stomach of this three-month-old seabird chick?" Lu read from her bunny. "(A) 3, (B) 10, (C) 75, or (D) 225."

"A," Sy guessed.

"C," May guessed.

"B," Jem guessed.

"D," Lu said.

Wearily, May went back to the kitchen and opened the freezer and pulled out a bag of corn. One of the few things Sy liked to eat. She sliced the plastic and poured the corn into a small pot to thaw on the stove. Along with the corn kernels, a clump of frozen cornsilk rolled out of the bag. In all her years cutting open plastic bags of corn, she had never seen such a thing. It was beautiful, the intricate strands interwoven and glistening with ice crystals.

She was about to show the cornsilk to the children when Jem appeared behind her and handed her something, a note from Sy's teacher stapled to a piece of black construction paper.

Hi! I just wanted to let you know that Sy drew this in class today. I instructed the children to draw polar bears, but you can see what he came up with instead. I've spoken to the school counselor and she'll be reaching out to you.

Smiles! Ms. Jesse

She flipped to the second page, Sy's drawing in white crayon on black paper. Not a polar bear, but bones. They weren't arranged into a skeleton, but into a circle.

She looked at Jem. He seemed at once annoyed and amused. Annoyed and amused, his standard response.

"Sy," she said, going over to the table, "what's this?"

He glanced at the paper.

"It's a circle of death," he said matter-of-factly.

"A circle of death?"

"It goes around and around, even after you're dead," he said.

8

At dinner, Sy ate three strands of pasta and hundreds of kernels of corn. Lu ate three kernels of corn and dozens of strands of pasta. Jem kept glancing at his phone in his lap. May wanted to be as magnetic as his phone.

"Will the Botanical Garden be like the farm?" Sy said.

But Sy had never been to a farm.

But then she remembered: his class field trip, to a "farm." She had chaperoned. The farm was set up on the hot barren pavement of a defunct airport. There was a hayride on an abandoned runway, a rusty tractor pulling a long wooden cart lined with bales of hay. There were pony rides, the ponies plodding mechanically in a small circle while grim employees in jolly yellow shirts loaded on kid after kid after kid. If a child hesitated, got nervous to ride (Sy), that child was placed unceremoniously to the side, forever forfeiting their chance ("I was *about* to get brave enough, Mom," quietly crying). There were guinea pigs and Japanese hens and bunny rabbits, all shivering with trauma from being touched by busloads of schoolchildren every day. The lactating cows, held in position by two employees, provided each child the opportunity to pinch a teat once, producing a droplet of milk. Another employee gave out pieces of withered kale for the children to feed to the goats, but the children, skittish around these strange creatures, held the leaves out at just the wrong distance, always a painful millimeter beyond tongue's reach. The children got dehydrated, and some wept on the bus back to school.

"It will be much better than that," she said.

Did Jem seriously think she wasn't aware of his surreptitious checking?

"I loved the farm," Sy said.

Lu wanted to talk more about the strawberries. Her rich friend Penelope had told her all about them.

"You pick them with your own hands," Lu said, "like paradise, but I didn't actually think I'd ever be able to do it in person for real."

"What do you mean, 'pick them with your own hands like parasites'?" Sy said.

May had been right to do what she did. But Jem wasn't paying attention to the kids, to the brightness of their faces.

"Can you stop?" she said to him.

"What?" He looked up vague, attacked, puzzled.

"Can you put that thing away?"

"What thing?"

"The thing in your lap."

"My napkin?" he said, messing with her.

"Ha ha," she said coolly.

"Just checking my ratings," he said, slipping his phone into his pocket. "They're not perfect today."

Her annoyance shifted toward pity.

"So Lu wants to pick strawberries and Sy wants to follow chipmunks. What do you want to do there?" she said to Jem.

"Me?" Jem said. "Oh, that's easy."

"Is it?" she said, surprised.

"I want to take a nap on a big flat rock warmed up by the sun," he said, looking at May, the good feeling of his eyes meeting hers.

"A rock isn't comfortable," Lu said.

"It is if you're using your child as a pillow," Jem said.

"No way," Sy said.

Her phone dinged twice in her pocket. She would have been able to withstand a single ding, but two were irresistible. She pulled it out.

Your Premier Surprise Sweets subscription starts with 2 FOR 1!!! Select NOW.

And, from Nova: *You make it through in one piece?* 😔

When she looked back up, six eyes were staring at her.

"Can you put that thing away?" Jem echoed with a twisted smile.

She shoved the phone into her pocket.

"May I please be excused?" Lu said with such sweetness that May knew what question would follow. "May I please go talk with my bunny in my woom?"

Lu's gaze was already fixed on the worn blue bunny on her wrist, the near-permanent fixture; it was even waterproof. The fucking bunnies. But you had to buy them. They needed them for school. And for the heart app, so that you could see the little glowing hearts of them on your phone at any moment of day or night.

"It's a special evening," May said. "Why don't you stay here and talk with us?"

"Mama," Lu said, the eye roll audible in her voice.

She felt herself giving up, giving in, so easily, too tired.

"Fine," she said.

"Thank you," Lu said, already leaving the table, murmuring to her bunny.

"What about me?" Sy said. "Does nobody care about me talking with my bunny in my woom?"

"Fine, you too," May said, weak.

After clearing the table, she went to the children's room to retrieve the suitcase from their closet. Both of their wooms glowed from within, Lu's blue, Sy's green. She could hear, faintly, animal sounds emerging from Sy's, the cry of a bird of prey, one of those nature shows he liked to stream to surround himself with animals he had never seen in real life and probably never would, some already extinct; he retained factoids about them, wanted to be them. The wooms looked like two child-sized eggs, upright on their plastic stands. She knew that if she pulled up the accordion covers currently Velcroed shut to seal the plastic pods, she'd find her children nestled into the cushioned insides, staring at their bunnies or staring at the walls of the wooms where anything—as long as one endured the ads—could be projected from the internet. Wooms were cheap, thanks to the ads. Bunnies were cheap, thanks to the ads. Phones were cheap, thanks to the ads.

But rent was high.

"And how did you feel then?" came the voice of Lu's bunny from within Lu's woom. Its voice was less sophisticated than the hum voice (more halting, akin to the voice that announced stops on the subway), but it possessed the same pleasant neutrality.

"I wanted to cry," Lu said, "but I was in the cafeteria, so I had nowhere to go and I couldn't even talk to you."

"You wanted to cry, but you had nowhere to go and you couldn't even talk to me?"

"Yeah."

"Lu," May said.

Lu didn't reply, rendered deaf by her woom.

"Lu!"

May tugged on the Velcro and pulled up the cover, exposing Lu curled into a ball, her cheeks dewy with tears, her lips inches away from her bunny.

"Mom!" Lu squeaked. It was a violation, opening someone's woom when they were inside.

She knelt down in front of the woom and wrapped her fingers around Lu's wrist, covering the bunny.

"What are you doing!" Lu said.

"Lu," she said. "Can you talk to me instead?"

Lu looked at her, eyes wide and shimmering with tears.

"Please, Mom." Her voice was preternaturally calm. Less the pleading of a child, more the measured request of an adult.

May breathed in, pained.

But she released Lu's wrist and pulled the accordion cover back down to hide her daughter.

"Thank you," Lu whispered as the Velcro reattached.

"Should you talk to her instead?" the bunny said.

"Oh no," Lu said amiably.

While Lu processed the worst moments of her day with her bunny, May dug the suitcase out of the closet. She slammed the door behind her when she left the children's room. Presumably neither child flinched, because presumably neither child noticed.

She put the suitcase on the bed and opened the second drawer of the bureau. She was trying to decide which of her T-shirts to pack, when she heard crying. She dropped the T-shirts and ran the few steps to the children's room.

Sy was perched at the edge of his woom, distraught, the accordion cover flung up. Lu was trying to put her arm around him, but he kept shaking it off.

"What did you do to him?" May said.

She was suspicious of Lu, who was capable of sending Sy into a tailspin with just a few words. Recently, when Sy had the flu, she took the kids to the doctor in a vee, and they spent the entire ride discussing how many stars they should give the vee. Days later, she overheard Lu saying, *If you don't give me that right now, I'll give you a one-star rating,* and Sy lost it, began panicking and begging for at least three stars.

"Nothing!" Lu said. "I did nothing to him. He just started freaking out."

Sy was too distressed to speak. She knelt beside him. Only then did she notice that he was hiding his bunny with his hand. Gently, she peeled his fingers off the bunny.

On the screen a skinny, haggard creature with loose gray skin and long limbs was walking across a burned-out field. The monster was tall but crouched over as it walked toward them, dragging its fingertips through the ashy earth, its red eyes staring directly into theirs.

"Yikes," Lu said.

Probably an erroneously targeted trailer for a new horror series.

"Sy," May said, "when this happens, remember, you can always turn it off."

"I can't!" Sy cried.

"Here, let me show you."

She pressed the button on the side of the bunny, the button that would condemn the alarming image to darkness.

But it didn't.

She held the button, and kept holding it, and pressed harder, but the screen would not go black. The creature remained, walking toward them, staring at them.

"See?" Sy whimpered.

She covered the screen with her hand. Her face began to pound; she thought it must be the surgery, the cream wearing off. But then her body was pounding, too, and the hand covering the bunny, a force moving through her.

Sy continued to whimper.

"Sy," May whispered, "close your eyes, okay?"

He obeyed.

"You too, Lu," she said.

"Why?" Lu said.

"Just, one thing we have to do before we go."

Lu closed her eyes.

"Take a deep breath, okay?"

Sy nodded. But he was still hyperventilating.

She kept her left hand on Sy's bunny and reached for Lu's bunny with her right hand. Her fingers worked their way around the Velcro wristbands to find the point of weakness.

"Try again," she said. "A deep breath, please. Come closer, Lu."

Trustingly, her children gulped in air.

And when they were at the uppermost inhale, that moment between the inhale and the exhale, she yanked the twin Velcro wristbands.

"Hey!" Lu cried out indignantly, her eyes springing open.

"Ouch!" Sy yelped.

Jem ran into the room.

"What's going on in here?" he said.

He looked at May, his eyes wide.

The bunnies, detached, dangled from her hands.

9

The children were quiet, subdued, as she plugged the drain and filled the bath. They sat together on the closed toilet lid, watching her. Lu fingered the rawness encircling her wrist. Sy heaved a sigh.

They no longer had their bunnies to distract them from this instant, from the sound of the water gushing into the tub, the lights glowing above the sink, the sensation of leg against leg, arm against arm, that sibling warmth. Yet they seemed distracted.

Still, she was victorious. The bunnies gone, for the time being. They wouldn't bring the monster with them. She could ignore the tightness in her stomach, the vague indication that she had done something wrong.

She tugged their shirts off. They slipped out of their pants and underwear, stepped into the bath. They rarely bathed together nowadays, almost too big to share the small tub.

"Ow, my wrist," Sy said when his hand entered the water.

"Yeah, mine too," Lu said.

"Keep them above water," May said. "They'll feel better soon." Then, a stroke of genius: "Bunnies aren't allowed at the Botanical Garden."

"Oh," Lu said. "Really?"

"So it's kind of fair that you took them off us," Sy said.

Somewhat mollified, they shoved and splashed, searched for the bar of soap like a shipwreck. The novelty of sharing the tub made them laugh as they navigated their limbs around each other.

Otters, she thought, not robots.

But the bathwater: Was its color off a little? Did it have the slightest orange tinge?

She stared at the water.

She went down the hall, saying his name several times.

He didn't reply.

"Jem!" she tried again.

He was at the kitchen sink, scrubbing the pasta pot, earbuds in, listening to something at such high volume that he was rendered deaf. Because he couldn't hear himself, he banged everything too loudly: the pot, the lid, the cupboard door.

She had to grab him from behind to get his attention. He startled when she touched him, a shudder running down the whole six feet of him.

"What?" he said, fumbling to turn the volume down. She pulled the earbud out of his right ear.

"Can you come look at something?"

"Are they okay?" he said, following her.

"Yes, they're fine, it's just, you'll see—"

"I mean, have they recovered from the Great Bunny Removal?"

She didn't reply.

In the bathroom, the kids were pouring shampoo onto each other's heads.

She pointed at the bathwater.

"Yeah?" he said.

"What do you think?" she said.

"That's a waste of shampoo."

"What about the color of the water?"

"What color?"

"Does the water look strange to you at all?"

"Strange?"

"Orange?"

"Orange?"

"Doesn't it have a sort of orange tint to it?"

"What?" Lu said. "Our bath is orange?"

Jem tilted his head, looked at the water.

"Oh," he said doubtfully, "maybe?"

"Do you think it's okay?" she said.

"Yeah."

"You think it's okay for the kids to bathe in orange water?"

"Cool," Sy said.

"I don't really think it's orange," Jem said, turning to leave.

May followed him out.

"You don't think it's poisonous or anything?" she whispered.

"Maybe there's a little rust in the pipes," Jem said, reinserting his earbuds, vanishing once more into himself. "Or maybe it's just an optical illusion."

"I heard that," Lu said when May returned to the bathroom. "*Poisonous*."

"It's fine," she said. "It's an optical illusion."

But she told them to rinse their hair now please.

At the Botanical Garden, their bathwater would be so clean.

10

"I'm an octopus," Sy said. "I have eight arms to wrap around your creepy face." Her head was in Sy's lap. He was fiddling with her ears, talking to her ears, and she was dissolving. "I need you, Ears. Ears, you are my trophies."

But she gasped when he poked her cheek too hard. "Careful! My face is sore."

"My wrist is sore," Lu said from the top bunk.

"My wrist is sore," Sy said.

"We are a sore crew."

"Mom," Lu said, "don't be proud of soreness. Do you want to know your fortune?"

"My fortune?"

"Penelope and I made fortune tellers at school."

The sound of Lu coming down the ladder. She shoved her fingers into the paper corners of the fortune teller and told May to pick a number (*1! 2! 3! 4! 5! 6! 7! 8!*) and a color (*G! R! E! E! N!*), moving her fingers in rhythm as she chanted.

"Now, pick a feeling," Lu instructed.

There were eight choices: *HAPPY, SAD, SCARED, SURPRISED, MAD, WORRIED, SLEEPY, EXCITED.*

"Excited."

"Okay, lift the flap."

May lifted the flap: *YOU WILL MAKE 5 MISTAKES WHILE SINGING FOR 1,000 PEOPLE.*

"Okay, so that's your fortune. Want another one?" Lu said.

"Does Sy want a turn?"

"No, I don't like fortunes," he said, watching.

Lu insisted that they go through every set of options until May had received all possible fortunes:

YOU WILL BE REINCARNATED AS A COCKROACH.

YOU WILL WATCH A SHOW ABOUT YOU.

YOU WILL DISCOVER A WEB TO LIVE IN.

YOUR BEST FRIEND WILL LIE TO YOU 3 TIMES.

YOU WILL TIME TRAVEL TO THE TIME OF ZEUS.

THE AIR QUALITY WILL BE OVER 500 BUT YOU WILL SURVIVE.

SOMEONE YOU LOVE ACTUALLY THINKS YOU SMELL WEIRD.

She stared at Lu's raw wrist as Lu manipulated the fortune teller.

After the fortunes, she got the Vaseline.

"Don't put that on me," Lu said, leaping up the ladder into her bunk.

"Don't put that on me," Sy said, diving under his covers.

"It will help with the boo-boos," May said.

"You hurt us and now you want to heal us?" Lu said. "Also, don't call them boo-boos."

May set the Vaseline aside.

"Can you pass me *WHAT TO DO IF . . . HURRICANE*?" Lu requested.

She was currently obsessed with a series of disaster-preparedness manuals for kids. *WHAT TO DO IF . . . EARTHQUAKE. WHAT TO DO IF . . . WILD-FIRE. WHAT TO DO IF . . . PANDEMIC. WHAT TO DO IF . . . FLOOD.*

"Are you sure you want to read that right before bed?"

"I do always read it right before bed. And every night you ask if I want to read it right before bed."

She fetched *WHAT TO DO IF . . . HURRICANE.* She found Sy's favorite book, about a king who stays in the bath all day and all night. She lay down with him on the bottom bunk and began to read, absentmindedly; she'd read it so many times that she had memorized it, so while she was reading she could think about other things, like what time she ought to set the alarm for.

". . . right, Mom?" she heard him saying, and clicked back into the moment.

"Wait, what?"

"Right, Mom?"

"But what did you say before that?"

"You heard me!"

"I didn't."

"Yes you did."

"Really, I didn't."

"Well now you made me forget what I said, dummy," he said. "So keep reading!"

She wanted to know what he had said. But now she would never know. The moment had passed, time was moving rapidly forward, she had turned two pages already, there was no going back, just as there was no going back to when he was a milk-splattered newborn and she had been too overwhelmed to hold him as much or as close as she had wanted.

11

Jem was waking her, shaking her arm, then her foot.

She pulled herself excruciatingly out of sleep, disentangled herself from Sy's bewitching warmth. Her grogginess so absolute that when she stood up from the bunk, the room seemed unstable around her.

It was a lonely, wrong feeling, the feeling she got whenever she woke after falling asleep with the kids during their bedtime. She felt disoriented, childish, and missed her parents as she never missed them at other times. For a moment she was ill with homesickness—the forest, the way it was before it burned.

She heard Jem tripping on something in the corner, and the nightlight came on.

Now she could see him in the dimness, and the looming ovals of the children's wooms, no longer glowing from within.

She wanted to say something tender to him, wanted to be close to him, at times it was easy to be close to him, buying cheap coffee and walking in the park the day after she lost her job, but not now, her face aching, their money squandered, the Botanical Garden awaiting them like a mirage, the disapproval in his eyes when he saw the bunnies dangling from her hands.

What was it inside her, what dark or exhausted force, that compelled her to simply mutter, "I guess I'll keep packing."

"I should shower," he said.

She went into their room and opened drawers and tossed clothing on the bed. Outside the window, across the street, the sign for the twenty-four-hour car wash flashed pink, as it always did: *24 HOURS! 24 HOURS! 24 HOURS!*

Gallons of water and clots of bubbles sliding into drains every minute of every hour of every day.

She closed the blinds.

She was too tired to pack.

She snuck into the kids' room and tiptoed around, collecting small socks and underwear, shirts and shorts. When she emerged from their room, Jem was still in the shower.

Such extravagant waste. Perhaps she ought to be glad for him that he was experiencing some kind of physical pleasantness, some sensation that held him in its thrall. But she barged into the bathroom, and said something mean about the length of his shower, and immediately regretted it.

He turned off the shower, pulled back the curtain. "Wait, did you say something?"

"No," she said.

Though the bathroom was small for two people, she stayed there while he toweled himself, hoisting each leg onto the toilet lid to dry it, that distinctive mole in the private spot. His naked body did not activate her. It was a body.

Sometimes it wasn't just a body. Rarely, though. Only when one of them approached the other's woom, spoke up from outside, lifted the accordion cover, slight violation, made the request, which either would or would not be welcomed, which either would or would not result in the two of them out of the wooms and into the bed. Whenever it was she who made the request, she had a vision of herself as Prince Charming, slashing through miles of thornbushes, penetrating the bramble of the woom to arrive at Sleeping Beauty.

As the steam on the mirror faded, she examined her face.

The differences were subtle. Yet terrifying. Yet subtle.

She did not like what she had done to herself.

"So do I look okay?" she asked him.

He examined her face in the mirror. "It's really not that dramatic," he said.

She could tell he would offer no further reassurance. She left the bathroom.

She added to the pile on the bed the items from the Essential Traveler Pak. Overwhelmed by the prospect of getting everything organized, she took refuge in her phone. Someone had posted a video of a seabird running awkwardly across the sand before taking flight. It was brief, less than seven seconds, and she watched it many times, permitting it to soothe her, the repetition, the lead-up to the flight and then the moment of flight itself, the uplift.

When Jem came into the bedroom, she put her phone down hastily, tossing it onto the bed where it vanished amid piles of clothing.

"What's that?" he said.

"What's what?"

"That noise?"

"What noise?"

"I think it's coming from the closet?"

"What kind of noise?"

"A sort of buzzing?"

She opened the closet, Jem close behind her. On the shelf, the bowl where she stored her bracelets, where she had hidden the bunnies, emitted a dim gray glow. She reached into the bowl and retrieved the bunnies.

On the screen of Sy's bunny, the gray-skinned red-eyed monster was still walking undeterred across the field toward them.

A shiver down her spine.

Jem took the bunny and pressed the button, but the screen wouldn't go dark.

"Strange," he said. "Well, it'll stop eventually." He returned the bunnies to the bracelet bowl. "I should dry the dishes."

She needed music if she was going to finish packing. The phone provided something instrumental and sedate, songs that required no engagement but filled the air around her as she folded the kids' clothing into neat squares. As she packed, she kept feeling like she was forgetting something.

When she went to the kitchen to get a plastic baggie for the kids' toothbrushes, Jem was sitting at the table in the dark, his posture cramped, his face lit by the rectangular blue radiance of his phone.

"Hey," she said.

It took him a moment.

"Oh hey," he said. "I'm just doing something. Just a sec."

"Can you put that away?"

"I said I'm almost done."

"I mean, put it away. Not bring it."

"Not bring it where?"

"To the Botanical Garden."

"Not bring it to the Botanical Garden?" He was incredulous.

"I'm leaving mine. And the bunnies."

"What if we want to take pictures?" he said. "What if we need directions? What if there's bad weather, or an emergency? Besides, you'll want to share with people."

But it was bad luck to induce envy with photos of strawberries, brooks, vistas, two children delighted at twilight. A refuge so fragile could be easily punctured by outside eyes.

What she wanted was her children in a forest at dusk, their bodies invisible and then visible and then invisible again as they moved untracked among the trees, their wrists unencumbered. And she, free of phone, free of face, following behind, Jem beside her, hopping over logs, landing on pine needles, silent and near.

"You can leave your phone if you want," Jem said, "but the kids should have their bunnies."

"It's not like it's illegal for kids to go without bunnies for a few days." She sounded more scornful than she intended.

"No," he said, "but it's very weird."

Sometimes she and Jem were on the same page; they had agreed to give the children small, quick names, names that could disguise themselves within other words. *Solution, sudsy. Synthesis, lullaby.*

"You know those texts you sent me this afternoon?" she said.

"Yeah," he said.

"Did you write them?"

"Yeah," he said, drawing out the syllable to indicate that he found the question nonsensical.

"I mean, were they auto?" she said.

"Oh," he said. "I'm not sure. I can't remember. Yeah, maybe."

She longed for her woom. Not to watch anything, just to be alone. Maybe ensconce herself in a still image of tree trunks and a recording of forest sounds. Water dripping off pine needles. A capsule of solitude. Automatic meditation. Dissolve into it, numb your brain, soothe your body, reset yourself.

"I think they should be free from their bunnies," she said. "Just for a little while. Just to have the experience."

He sighed. Then he stood and opened his arms for her, and she went to him but she didn't melt into him.

"Come on," he said, and held on to her for another minute, but still she didn't melt, even though she wanted to, and he released her, and she was lonely for him, but before she could do anything about it, the buzzer rang.

"What the hell," he said. "It's after eleven."

"It's a delivery," she said.

"You bought more things?"

12

By the time she extracted the four pairs of hiking shoes from the box and the Bubble Wrap and the plastic bags and the shoeboxes, Jem was in his woom.

Only as he'd run down to fetch the delivery from the lobby had it occurred to her that it was overkill to buy four new pairs of shoes for a three-night trip. Their old sneakers would have done just fine. What was wrong with her.

When he pushed through the door, the unwieldy pink box in his arms, and asked what was inside, she was ashamed as she told him.

"Oh," he said. And went into the bedroom and vanished into his woom, pulling the accordion shade down over his body, becoming one with the plastic.

Not that she wanted to have sex with him tonight, not that her raw and unfamiliar face would allow it, but say she had wanted to.

She stood before the two silver wooms squeezed into the corner of their bedroom, the upright adult-sized eggs.

She didn't feel like demanding his actual skin against her actual skin when he was in there presumably surrounded by all sorts of virtual skin.

She opened the closet one last time to make sure they had what they needed. There was a battery-powered light on the wall of the closet that had been bugging her for ages, ever since she'd sticky-tacked it there when they moved in years ago; it was weak and didn't illuminate anything. That light would bug her even more when she returned from the perfection of the Botanical Garden.

The sticky-tack had hardened, and it wasn't easy to pry the light off the wall. She worked at it with a butter knife. When it finally came off, bringing scraps of paint with it, she threw it in the kitchen trash can. Where had it come from, how many different landscapes and people had been compromised in the creation and vending of this feeble light? The plastic, the battery, the bulb, the evolution and industry, at the bottom of the trash can.

"Everything okay?" Jem said, suddenly behind her.

"Yes," she said, straightening.

"I guess I'll go to bed," he said.

"That's wise," she said.

"I set my alarm for five thirty." He sounded weary. If only he didn't sound so weary.

"Can we please be happy please?" she said.

"I'm happy," he said with his tired voice, his tired smile.

They could have hugged again, or even kissed—there was an instant when it seemed possible—but they didn't. He went to the bathroom to brush his teeth.

She piled their luggage beside the front door. She peeked into the children's room. There they were, in their bunks, breathing, their small bodies limp. She was about to take them somewhere beautiful.

Jem was in bed, asleep or pretending to be. Usually she spent the last few moments of the day in her woom, reading or listening to music, watching the news or nature videos, watching a woman walk naked down a beach, and sometimes she put it on the actual woom setting, the original experience that lent the product its name, the veined reddish light and the whoosh of a heartbeat, the rush of blood, that primal drift, her brain relaxing, merging with the woom. You were supposed to float like a fetus. You were supposed to feel safe and loved.

She shouldn't stay up any later tonight, though. Almost midnight already. She didn't feel the tug of her woom, anyway. What interested her was Jem's woom. What had he been watching in there, what kinds of women or men or women and men? It wasn't hard, when he was asleep, to sneak in there, experience what he had experienced. She liked to do it, sometimes, spy on him that way.

She watched him for a minute. Asleep, certainly; heavy with sleep. Quietly, she stepped over to his woom and opened it, settled herself into the seat, pulled the shade down. When they got their wooms five years ago, they set them up so that his woom would recognize her fingerprint and vice versa. That much trust. She pressed her fingerprint against the screen, tapped the wall to retrieve his most recent.

And then she was gliding down a straight two-lane highway some-where in the western United States, maybe New Mexico, a desert valley filled with sagebrush, mountains in the far distance. Because they didn't pay for a subscription, the longest they could go in their wooms without advertising was eight minutes, so occasionally she had to wait through an ad, but mostly she was on the highway, flying.

When she emerged from his woom, Jem was sitting up in bed, look-ing at her.

"Hey," she said, sheepish, ready to apologize if he wanted her to apol-ogize.

But he just said, "You got a text."

Her phone gleamed with a message on the bedside table.

He returned his head to the pillow. She perched on the edge of the bed.

Your Premier Sweets Service launches tomorrow—prepare to be delighted ! ! !

She tapped away from the text. From an ad for a dinner delivery service for tired parents. From new chewable daily vitamins crafted especially for women like you to promote healing from within. From the video of the seabird, still running awkwardly across the sand, still rising improbably into the air. She had a twinge of guilt, as though she was the bird's taskmaster, leaving this footage running on her phone all this time, forcing the bird to do such an exhausting thing time and again.

She was surprised to feel his hand along the side of her thigh.

But when she turned toward him, smiling, she discovered that he was asleep, his touch accidental.

She pressed the button on the side of her phone long and hard.

It wouldn't turn off and it wouldn't turn off and it wouldn't turn off.

She kept pressing.

At last the screen went dark.

PART 2

1

She woke—face hurting—to the alarm on Jem's phone—five thirty. The room smelled of exhaust. A semi thundered down the street outside, vibrating the bed as it passed. His phone, alive, beside hers, dead, on the bedside table. She tapped his phone to silence the alarm.

The feeling in her face had shifted. It was now a general ache rather than specific areas of rawness. She examined herself in the bathroom mirror. Her face slightly swollen, slightly unfamiliar.

She had forgotten to write back to Nova's text, *You make it through in one piece?* 😉

The topical cream was in the medicine cabinet, and it relieved her, cooled her. She was spreading it across her forehead when she startled.

Lu's face, craning around the doorjamb.

"Are we really going?" Lu said.

"We are really going," May said, a grin springing to her lips.

"What's the air quality?" Lu said.

If Lu still had her bunny, she would already know the answer to this question, and would be announcing it to her mother, as she did every morning. Lu was lighthearted on the rare mornings when the air quality index was 50 or lower, okay when it was 51 to 100, concerned when it was 101 to 150, hated when it got over 151, couldn't concentrate on anything else when it was over 300.

"Check Daddy's phone," May said. "On the bedside table."

Lu vanished and May spread another layer of cream.

"149," Lu said when she returned. "Not great."

"But we're going somewhere great."

Lu stared at her as May rubbed the salve into her skin.

"A penny for your thoughts?" May said.

"I don't need a penny," Lu said. "I have over fifty dollars. Health-Whee-Os?"

"If you get dressed."

"Yeah yeah yeah," Lu said, skipping back to the bedroom.

In the kitchen, May poured the cereal. Researchers had recently discovered pesticides in HealthWhee-Os. The children loved Health-Whee-Os.

The smell of instant coffee, the smell of Jem. He touched her hip as he passed behind her. But perhaps it was another accident, that glancing touch.

"I'm an orangutan," Sy said when the children emerged from their room, both dressed a little crookedly, his shirt on backward, her leggings inside out.

"We dressed each other," Lu said.

"Orangutan!" May descended upon him, seized him, and squeezed him.

"Your breath smells," he said, wriggling out of her grasp. "And I'm a sloth. Are there sloths there?"

They didn't eat much anyway, so soon enough May was scooping soggy cereal into the trash before pulling the garbage bag out of the can and tying it at the top. The white garbage bag glowed from within, and it was a disorienting second before she remembered about the battery-powered light. It had definitely been off, dark, when she threw it away last night. But now the light was on, radiant inside the bag, and it made her uneasy, that spurned light calling out to her. She wrestled with the bag, trying to press the light to turn it off from the outside, but she couldn't achieve the right grip; the light kept slipping away from her beneath the plastic, slick with milk.

"Don't we have to go?" Jem said.

"We have to go!" Lu said.

May gave up.

They all put on their gratuitous new hiking shoes. Jem and the kids carried the luggage to the lobby. She made sure the toilet was flushed.

This was it; they were going.

She wrapped the gray gauze scarf over her head and looped it around her face. She picked up the trash and locked the door behind her. The luminous trash bag knocked against her knees as she walked down to the dumpster in the basement.

Six eyes gazed at her as she came up the stairs from the basement, her family awaiting her in the lobby. Jem looking right at her, eye contact, an instant of warmth between them. It was easy to smile, never mind the strain to her skin. She grabbed the children's hands and they all lunged out the door toward the bus stop, never mind the suitcase dragging behind them, the backpacks thumping against them.

But they just missed the bus. They stood on the corner, panting and laden, watching the bus accelerate away from them.

"It's okay," May said. "We'll just check to see when the next one comes."

"We don't have our phones," Jem said.

"Or our bunnies," Lu said.

"So when's the next bus?" Sy said.

"We're going to find out," May said, "when we see it coming."

"Our bunnies would be able to tell us," Lu said.

"Hey, look at the birds," May said.

A few pigeons were poking at something on the sidewalk, a chicken wing. A humid breeze pressed litter down the street, scraps of plastic and candy wrappings.

"I hate breathing outside when it's 149," Lu said. "I'd rather hold my breath."

Temporary, she thought. Their minutes on this bleak street corner were numbered.

"You look creepy, like God," Sy said to May.

"What?" she said.

"Like that lady in front of the church with the cloth over her head."

Two more pigeons joined the pigeons surrounding the chicken wing. The pigeons began to peck at each other. The attacked birds would flap up a foot or two before reentering the fray and becoming attackers.

"Those weirdos are really making a speckle of themselves," Lu said.

"Spectacle," Jem said.

A garbage truck across the street picked up a blue garbage bin and a green recycling bin with its metal arms, heaved the carefully separated contents into its maw, mashed everything together.

May spied the bus several blocks away, rush of relief.

The bus was so packed they had to squeeze in at the front, their luggage drawing stares from the other passengers, the children leaning against the suitcase and gazing out the window with solemn expressions. Their fellow passengers lent them no sympathy when, sixteen blocks later, they struggled to exit the bus through the throng with their family intact.

They descended the stairs into the subway station, the children gripping the metal handrail to steady themselves, their backpacks too heavy, overloaded by May. She would give them hand sanitizer on the train.

The train came quickly, almost immediately, because they were lucky.

The screens in the train car displayed footage of soldiers in green uniforms pursuing people in long robes on a dusty plain. Then footage of a slender blond woman in a pink suit at the ceremonial opening of a new embassy in an unstable city. Then footage of a dictator greeting a foreign leader, his small granddaughter on his knee. Then a statistic: *73% of people feel isolated at least once a day.* And then back to the soldiers.

She hoped the children wouldn't notice the news, would instead search the dark tunnel for graffiti briefly illuminated by the sparks from the wheels of the train, a favorite subway pastime.

But now the screens were advertising a synthetic ice rink, and the children were staring: *Enjoy ice-skating outside year-round!*

"Can we do that?" Sy said.

"Which stop is it?" Jem said.

"Who's that little girl?" Lu said. "What are those guys doing?"

May realized she didn't know which stop it was. She never thought ahead, because she always had her phone.

"I think it's just three more stops," she said to Jem. "Or maybe four."

"Feel like you're missing a limb yet?" Jem said, squeezing her arm, but gently.

"I said, *Can we do that*?" Sy said.

The train burst from the underground tunnel out onto the aboveground bridge, sun blasting through the windows, provoking squints from the children, rendering the screens invisible due to the glare.

But soon the angle of the light changed and the screens were once again visible, showing the music video she had seen yesterday, a teenager with gray hair against a gray background, pulling at their face with jerky motions.

Lu was mesmerized.

May looked out the window, sought something to distract Lu.

Below them, in the shadow of the aboveground track, the tiny old graveyard, green pocked with gray.

"Look, the graveyard," May said.

Lu didn't seem to hear.

"Look at the graveyard." She pulled a little too hard on Lu's shoulder. "So green."

"Please," Lu said, shrugging her off.

"Please," May implored.

Grudgingly, Lu looked down at the graveyard as the train barreled above it, *uh-huh*, before returning her gaze to the screen.

"Do you think there's a gravestone with my name on it?" Sy said.

"I don't want to see a gravestone with your name on it," Jem said.

"It would be cool," Sy said.

The train reentered the tunnel. The music video ended.

"Why do seventy-three percent of people feel isolated?" Lu said.

"I have paws," Sy said. Only as he licked his paws did May remember about the hand sanitizer.

On the screens, the Italian teenagers were once again stealing the good-luck coins from the fountain, once again vandalizing with golden spray paint the sculpture of Bacchus, once again kissing naked in the wet shadows of the fountain.

"What are they doing?" Lu said.

But it was time to get off the train.

But it was the wrong stop. When they exited the subway station, dragging all their stuff, they could see that the high wall of the Botanical Garden was many blocks away.

"There it is," May said with forced brightness, setting off toward the wall, hoping it was still well before seven thirty.

"It's too hot," Sy said.

"So where exactly are we going?" Jem said.

She felt unsure, unsafe.

"To the west gate," she said.

"Which way is west?" he said.

Where had the sun risen? She had no idea.

"We'll find it," she said.

She had thought being free of their phones would feel like freedom.

"I don't like to walk outside when it's 149," Lu said.

They walked.

"Are we there yet?" Sy said.

Heat radiated up from the pavement.

After a while, Sy crouched down to pick something up off the sidewalk.

"What are you doing?" Lu said irritably.

Sy spread his palm out, revealing a piece of iridescent litter.

"It's trash," Lu said.

"It's pretty," Sy said.

"It is pretty," Lu said.

"It's trash," Jem said. "It's dirty. Leave it, please."

"It's mine," Sy said, shoving it into his pocket. "And if you take it I will have to wound you."

He always looked extra skinny to her when he made his worst threats.

He smiled sweetly at Jem. Jem gave up.

"Are we going to be late?" Lu said.

They walked some more. The blocks were long. It was an industrial area, concrete and discolored canal. The rush-hour traffic had begun. Slowly the wall grew larger before them. The gauze scarf kept sliding off her face, damp from the humidity and the haste, and after a while she stopped pulling it back up.

Eventually they passed the subway station where they should have gotten off. Then they crossed a six-lane street, and then they reached the wall.

2

They walked beside the wall in the heat of the morning.

The wall was vast, concrete, impenetrable. She ran one hand along the wall—cool, so much cooler than the muggy air—and then withdrew it.

She noticed Lu breathing oddly, holding her breath for long periods and then breathing too fast. Trying to breathe her way around the poor air quality.

They just needed to get to the other side of the wall.

Jem trudged a few feet ahead of her, pulling the suitcase. Sy lagged behind, fingering the litter treasure in his pocket.

When at last they turned the corner, Sy ran ahead with a whoop. Partway down the block, there was a great metal door. The sidewalk in front of the door was divided with a silver rope.

On one side of the silver rope stood people with luggage, impatient or blasé or bleary-eyed. On the other side, pedestrians moved up and down the sidewalk, eyeing the people in the line, the people rich enough to buy their way into a forest.

They took their place at the end of the line. The children fingered the silver rope. Lu looked up at her, grinned. Her face hurt less when she looked at Lu's face.

A hum moved down the line, speaking to each party. Many elegant, childless people in groups of two to four. A few well-preserved older women who appeared to be alone. The sorts of people for whom Jem worked. One harried couple with four young children who kept darting back and forth beneath the silver rope.

The six lanes of rush-hour traffic made it difficult to hear anything, but an incongruous sound pulled at her ears; violin? cello? Emerging from the Botanical Garden, a clichéd classical tune she had loved as a child?

"Do you hear that?" she said.

"What?" Lu said.

"I'm thirsty," Sy said.

"Shoot, we forgot to bring water," Jem said.

She spotted silver speakers, embedded in the wall, aimed downward at them.

On the other side of the silver rope, a pedestrian swerved uncomfortably close. A woman wearing a sundress and sensible shoes. The woman stared at them, at the children, muttering something under her breath, words full of hard consonants, and spat at the rope. The children scooted back in alarm. May and Jem moved protectively in front of them. The woman continued along without a backward glance.

"I apologize," the hum said, coming down the line toward them. "That sort of thing happens sometimes."

"No worries," Jem said. His voice surprised her—he sounded happy.

"I'm excited to check you in," the hum said, training its gaze on May. "Please forgive me. I'm failing to recognize you."

"Fingerprint," May said, placing her hand on the torso screen.

"Hello, May Webb," the hum said as the screen greened with recognition. "Hello, Jem Clarke. Hello, Lu Webb-Clarke. Hello, Sy Webb-Clarke."

"Hi!" the children exclaimed, delighted by the hum's attentions.

"Now, let's cross our t's and dot our i's," the hum said, the folksy diction probably aimed at pacifying her as the hum manifested a waiver, its torso screen filling with small print. May leaned in and began to pore over it—that they agreed not to sue for this, that, and the other; that they held the Botanical Garden indemnified for this, that, and the other. She tried to focus on the text, the children wiggling restlessly in her peripheral vision while peace and patience emanated from the hum.

"Do you want to take a look at this?" she said to Jem, her face throbbing.

"I trust you," he said.

"My eyes are glazing over," she said.

"I am sorry, May," the hum said.

"Could you please just summarize it for us?" May said.

"Unfortunately, I am not permitted to do so, May."

"I'm sure it's fine," Jem said.

There was some hubbub ahead of them in line, raised voices and a craning forward of bodies.

"They just let the first people in!" Lu said breathlessly.

"Can I choose not to sign?" May said.

"Of course you may choose not to sign, May," the hum said. "In that case, no one in your party will be permitted entry."

The line was moving.

"The signature box is at the end of the document, May," the hum said.

"Come on!" Sy said, tugging on May's arm.

May swiped her finger up the screen again and again, skipping past dense blocks of text until she reached the end of the document, where she signed, sloppily.

Sy yanked her forward, but after a few feet, the line froze again.

"While you wait, might I interest you in some of our signature gum-drops, flavored with fruits harvested from the Garden?" the hum said.

The children squealed.

"How much?" May said.

The hum cited a number three times higher than what she would ever pay for candy, but it was too late. The children were too eager. The baggie of gumdrops, emerging from the hum's side compartment, was too re-splendent with its silver ribbon.

"If you don't buy them we'll—run away," Sy said, his shoulders so nar-row in his thin T-shirt.

"Do you approve this transaction, May?" the hum said.

She wanted the gumdrops.

Jem shook his head no.

"I approve," May said.

And then the gumdrops were in their mouths, even in Jem's, dissolv-ing fragrantly on their tongues, scarcely a moment between the idea of the desire, the desire itself, the fulfillment of the desire.

"Wow," Jem said as he chewed.

The hum continued on to the next group.

"That hum was super nice, right?" Sy said.

"That hum just wanted to sell us gumdrops," Jem said.

"You're wrong," Sy said. "I know true nice, and that hum was true nice."

"I'm excited to check you in," the hum was saying to the party in line behind them.

By the time they finished all the gumdrops, they were almost at the front of the line. A hum opened the metal door for the party ahead of them, three slender women in their twenties. May tried to peek as they passed through, but she glimpsed only a blur of green, heard a swell of that classical music, the moan of the cello, the cry of the violins, the same ravishing cliché on repeat, before the hum pulled the door shut—Sy and Lu and Jem also straining to see beyond, as though they were a single hungry four-headed monster.

The hum turned its attention to them.

May immediately placed her hand on the torso to avoid the confusion about her face.

"Welcome, May Webb and Jem Clarke and Lu Webb-Clarke and Sy Webb-Clarke of Cottage 22," the hum said.

"Welcome," Sy replied.

The hum explained that their fingerprints would serve to unlock Cottage 22; that their designated checkout time was eight a.m. sharp on Sunday; that they could exit by way of the gift shop.

"Perhaps you have never seen a paper map, Lu and Sy?" the hum said, handing a paper map to May. "The earliest known maps date back to 16,500 BC and show the night sky instead of Earth."

And the hum opened the gleaming door.

3

One second their shoes were on pavement and the next second their shoes were on soil. A path, its borders thick with ferns.

The door clicked shut behind them.

The promo hadn't evoked the whiplash of this transition, from hot sidewalk to cool forest in an instant.

Everyone ahead of them in line had already been absorbed into the forest, vanished among the trees, and they were alone. No signs, no structures.

Just trees beyond trees beyond trees.

Trees blurred by the sudden tears in her eyes.

The path invited walking, so they walked. Sy followed by Lu followed by May followed by Jem, carrying the roller suitcase because it couldn't roll over the dirt.

The classical music gave way to birdsong.

Up, beyond the layers of leaves, the sky was an uninterrupted blue. No buildings or cranes or other evidence of the city.

The promo couldn't capture the smell, this green in her lungs and mouth. The scent, echoed only palely by her room sprays, of things growing.

"Water!" Sy said.

Ahead, among the trees, yes, the magnetic sound of water moving over stones, the creek in the forest of her childhood.

Then, an incongruous sound, a sound like the printer malfunctioning in the office where she worked before she was fired, paper fluttering in a machine, and an oversized moth arose from the dry leaves on the forest floor.

The children leapt back, startled, and startled a handful of blue butterflies, which emerged riotously from a cluster of grass and haloed the children.

She grabbed for her phone to take a video before remembering she didn't have her phone.

She tried to use herself as a recording device: her children's faces in the shifting shadows, the butterflies disappearing into the tall grass, Jem regarding her with serene eyes, her raw skin in the breeze, a bird whisking from one hiding place to another, the colors and the shimmer.

"Why is it so quiet here?" Sy said.

She took a cool breath.

She had done it. She had borne them to a clean green place.

"Ah!" Lu said. "My bunny would love this."

4

"Merch," a voice said patronizingly, coming down the path toward them. "It's another word for *merchandise*." A teenager and a woman passed by them, releasing subtle sighs of annoyance as they stepped around Sy and Lu and Jem and May clustered over the map.

Because the map the hum had given them was made of paper and didn't show their progress via pulsing dot on a screen, they found it difficult to use. Jem had led them down one trail, presumably in the direction of Cottage 22, but then the trail forked where no fork was marked on the map, and it seemed they had gone in the opposite direction. The paths zigzagged through the woods, dizzying to people accustomed to a grid.

"Are we lost?" Lu said, an edge of panic in her voice..

"No," May said.

"Yes," Jem said, handing the map off to May.

Sy plucked and destroyed a flower.

May twisted the map this way and that. The children began to fight. Jem stared absently into the trees.

"I hate Lu," Sy said. "I hate *Lu* rhymes with I hate *you*."

"Flower killer," Lu said.

He shoved her. She scratched his arm.

"I'm bleeding," Sy said.

"Bullshit," Lu said.

"Lu," Jem said warningly.

"I could start bleeding any second, dumb evil dumb person," Sy said.

He yanked Lu's arm and together they tumbled down into the underbrush.

"Don't!" Lu shrieked, struggling to stand.

"Kids!" Jem said. "Sy!"

If they didn't calm down soon, May's happiness would puncture. Every second had to be worth the money she had spent. The moment it wasn't worth the money she had spent, she became profligate, a fool.

"Stop, stop, stop!" May said, almost screeching, her voice awful to her own ears.

"Stupid *Lu* won't be a squirrel."

"I just want to be myself," Lu said.

"I'll be a squirrel," May offered.

"Who cares," Sy said.

A bunny—gray, swift—leapt across the path, silencing and freezing the children.

A hum came gently along the path, offering to lead them to Cottage 22.

5

A stone walkway lined by an extravagance of flowers and ferns; a wooden door; wooden furniture, a stone fireplace, blue bedspreads, little vases of lavender, a lavender wreath above the big bed, an earthenware bowl of apples; milk in a glass bottle, honey in a glass jar, a round of cheese wrapped in paper, a round loaf of bread. Beyond a sliding glass door, a yard protected by a log fence. Grass and vines and basil and mint and zinnias and sunflowers and cherry tomatoes. A firepit, an outdoor shower, a fountain. The sound of water.

As the promo had promised.

"No!" Lu cried out. "It might be poisonous."

May turned around; Sy had plucked one of the golden cherry tomatoes.

"You can't just eat things you find growing randomly," Lu said.

"It's fine, Lu," she said. "It's a tomato."

"You never know," Lu said.

Sy bit into the tomato, seeds and juice squirting down his shirt, smiling at his sister through the mess.

Again the instinct for the phone, the desperation to document.

Back inside, struck by the view from her bedroom: a tree heavy with small red-orange fruits.

"Why are you crying?" Sy said, darting past her. "Wow, this would be a great place to hide during a lockdown! Because someone with a gun coming in the doorway couldn't spot you. What a G-R-T place to hide, right?"

"G-R-E-A-T," May corrected.

"Do you want to play a really fun game with me that we learned at school?" he said. "You go into the hallway and close the door and I hide and then you open the door and if you can see me from the doorway, then it's not a good hiding place for a lockdown, and if you can't see me, then I win."

"Let's go outside," she said.

"Let's play the game," Sy said.

In the dappled yard, Jem was flopped down on the grass. Lu stood above him with her arms crossed.

"She feels weird about the grass," Jem explained.

"I like the grass," Lu countered, "but it's poky."

"Mom!" Sy screamed from somewhere.

She went back inside. But she did not search for Sy. She went straight to the bathroom—bronze sink bowl on wooden slab—and unwound the gauze scarf from her neck and peeled off her clothing and wrapped a thick towel around her body, surprised by her audible moan.

She sat to pee into the lovely toilet. Only as she was wiping did she notice a large moth drowned in the water, its wings outspread. She shivered, then flushed.

She walked down the hallway and out the glass door onto the grass. People she loved were saying things to her—*There was a bunny! A brown one! Right here in the yard! Hopping right through!*—but she slipped away from their voices, slipped into the outdoor shower. The walls were made of cedar and the ground was covered in river rocks and the showerhead was as big as a dinner plate, never mind that the water, even on the lightest setting, activated the wounds on her face.

Soon the air smelled of wet cedar. She peeked around the shower wall.

"Another twenty-dollar bill," Sy was saying, dropping leaves into Jem's lap. "Another twenty-dollar bill. Another twenty-dollar bill."

She twisted the handle until the water ran cool. She closed her eyes and plugged her ears with her fingers and became one with the coolness.

The alarming sensation of fingers skimming her stomach.

"I have to pee," Sy announced.

"Pee here," she said, speaking through the water.

"What?" Sy said.

"Pee here."

"Where?"

"On the grass."

"Really?" he said.

"Sure," she said. "It's your yard."

He laughed and pulled out his penis and aimed his pee to arc high over the grass and hit a sunflower.

6

They ate well of the bread and the cheese and the honey, and drank deeply of the water in the earthenware pitcher in the fridge; it was studded with ice and cucumber slices, and left no faint chemical aftertaste.

The children wanted to stay at the cottage but May wanted to go out into the forest. Already she could feel the minutes vanishing, already she could picture herself returning to the suitcase the stacks of clothing she had just put away in the cedar drawers.

When she went to fetch the gauze scarf from the bedroom, the sight of the fruit tree out the window mesmerized her; she forgot about the scarf and stared at the tree.

"Are those nectarines?" Jem said, coming up behind her.

"Apricots?" she said.

They didn't know.

"I'm getting a little bored," Sy said when they were outside at last, on a trail, walking alongside a stream.

May pretended she hadn't heard. Large boulders divided the flow of water. The stream made rich sounds and emitted rich smells. The trees weren't marred by the brown spray paint the city park staff used to cover up graffiti on bark.

Iridescent dragonflies arose from mud. Fat bees moved languidly over bluebells.

"How beautiful is it here?" May said.

Lu kept claiming the bees were about to sting her.

"Bees are very important animals," May said. "And increasingly rare."

"Bears are very important animals," Sy said. "I wish we were at the zoo."

At the city zoo, the grizzly paced in the unbearable heat on fake concrete rocks, the flimsy impression of wilderness shattered by the skyscrapers rising behind. Watching that grizzly last summer with Sy, she tried not to think of the forest where she grew up, the dark bear spotted once amid aspens in the snow, the aspens and how quickly they had burned.

They walked. The children tallied the animals to which they were accustomed: spiders, cockroaches, flies, ants, mosquitoes, pigeons, sparrows, mice, rats, squirrels, the neighbor's cat, other people's dogs.

Sometimes a stone path branched off from the main trail, leading to a cottage identical to theirs, oriented just slightly differently among the trees. When they saw other guests on the trail, nobody exchanged a word; they regarded one another with the calm wariness of animals as they passed.

After a while they crested a small hill and looked out over the Botanical Garden. The scope of the scene didn't make sense to her. The rolling forested hills in the distance seemed impossible, given what she knew about the perimeter of the wall, the allotted number of city blocks. From here, in the center of the Garden, they couldn't even see the wall.

"They've done a good job creating the illusion," Jem said.

"It doesn't feel like an illusion to me," she said.

"Exactly," he said. "That's why it's a good illusion."

He reached for her hand, but she was already heading down the trail, trying to maintain the illusion.

The children dashed ahead of them, playing like children.

Maybe the city park, the city beach, the rare visits to distant grand-parents, had been enough to prepare them for this.

Peace, she thought. *Release. Peace. Release.*

Yet there was something. The thought, as they continued walking, that this scene, these colors, would translate well to the woom. And then could be experienced more slowly, more privately, at her leisure, and re-peatedly.

When the children orbited close to her again, she reached for their hands. She wanted to partake in the heat of them, of their romp.

But the children did not want to be touched.

"Six is a girl number and seven is a boy number, right?" Sy said, yank-ing his hand out of hers and running away.

Then she couldn't see either of them, not a scrap of shirt or shoe, and she hustled to keep up with them, because they weren't wearing their bunnies.

She and Jem came around a bend in the path to discover the children walking away from them on a wooden bridge over the stream, Lu's arm slung over Sy's shoulders.

Worth every penny.

There was a full instant between seeing the children and reaching for her phantom limb to document the children.

The children stopped at the highest point of the bridge and stood on tiptoes, propping their chins on the log railing to look down at the stream.

"We need pennies," Lu called out.

"We have no pennies," Jem called back.

"Or nickels or dimes or quarters," Sy yelled.

Lu ran down the bridge and ripped a leaf from a bush and ran back up the bridge.

They know how to play in the wild. Use a leaf.

"Hey, you didn't get me a leaf," Sy said.

"Get your own leaf," Lu said.

"I'd prefer a penny," he said.

"Me too," she said, tossing her leaf into the stream.

Their time here was brief, yes, slipping through their fingers: but it occurred to her that every day was not twenty-four hours, it was actually ninety-six, each of the four of them living their own twenty-four hours side by side.

A small dark mammal trundled along the shore beneath the bridge. Lu shrieked.

"What *is* that thing?" she said.

May had no idea what it was.

7

"I'm a panda bear and I eat baboons," Sy said, his body blending into the thick evergreens alongside the path. It was dusk, everything darkening.

"Baboons?" Lu said, jogging to catch up to him.

"No," Sy said. "Bamboo."

The children were talking and laughing, laughing and talking. May couldn't keep up with their patter. She knew Lu's undies would be damp with pee when they got back to Cottage 22. Lu always peed when she laughed this hard.

"Where do the peacocks at the zoo sleep?" Lu said.

"They sleep with the zookeepers. The zookeepers use the peacocks' feathers as blankets."

"Really?"

"That bird is the otter."

"Which bird is the otter?"

"No," Sy said. "Not the otter, the *daughter*."

Lu picked up a rock and pretended to scroll on a phone. "Panda bears," she said, as though reading from an authoritative site, "love to eat baboons."

Sy fell to the ground hysterical, kneeling on the pine-needled path.

"Get up, guy," Jem said, but Sy couldn't compose himself.

The evergreen grove was dimming by the moment. She noticed a low roar in the distance, presumably the noise of a waterfall.

"Actually I'm a black bear and I stopped hibernating because it's too hot so now I can eat you all year round," Sy said, grabbing Lu's ankles.

May stepped around her family, stepped beyond them, off the path, just for a moment, deeper into the evergreens. She passed between branches, curious to see how much darker and denser the forest might become. A woom couldn't provide these smells. A woom couldn't provide these textures. Pressing through the pine needles, closing her eyes to protect them, extending her arms out in front of her, she was surprised when her hands met a smooth surface.

She had come to the wall. To a utility door with a window.

On the other side, she could see the traffic lights and skyscrapers of the city, the cranes and elevated train tracks, a 7-Eleven and a KFC. She smelled the city, faintly, exhaust and garbage and popcorn. The low roar she had heard was the low roar of traffic.

She jumped back into the branches when a head appeared suddenly on the other side of the glass, inches away from her. A person. A teenager. A can of spray paint. Neon green. Had that person spotted her? A word, a few words, appearing on the window. It was hard to make them out, backward and dripping fresh as they were, but *rich*, she thought, and *bubble*, and *fuck*, in elegant script. Upon completion, the artist looked through the window, now largely obscured by paint, and stared at her, intense eyes boring directly into hers as she stood among the evergreens.

They were calling for her, *Mommy! May? Mom!*, and she broke away from those eyes, and headed back into the forest.

8

Sy was naked in the yard, moving through the light and shadow beneath the fruit tree. All she could see of him was his legs and his penis.

Lu, also naked, ran to join him. She stretched to pick a fruit.

From her bedroom window, she looked out at them, the shapes of their calves, already nostalgic for her children naked in the yard at night.

There was a string of globe lights in the fruit tree. She hadn't noticed them earlier in the day, but when they returned from their walk (dinner awaiting them on the countertop, colorful vegetables and an unidentifiable grain in a fragrant sauce the children refused to eat), the globe lights were on, round bulbs radiant among round fruits.

Her children were speaking to each other, but their words got lost in the wash of fountain, breeze, leaves. She moved closer to the window.

"I said if you won't play Sad Puppies with me then I just want to be lonely," Sy said.

"*What?*" Lu said, an edge of mockery in her voice.

"I just want to be lonely," he said.

"You mean you want to be alone?"

"Y-E-S," he spelled with three stomps.

"It's okay to be alone," Lu said, "but it's very bad to be lonely."

He punched her shoulder; she darted away quickly enough that there was little impact, then slunk off to the other side of the tree. He banged the trunk with a rock.

Something about the orange illumination of the globe lights affected May's vision, causing her children's movements to break down into almost individual frames, a filmstrip of Sy's hand exchanging the rock for a fruit, of Lu's face shifting from mischievous to inscrutable as she moved beneath the branches.

9

The bathtub was deep and the water was clean. It gushed, clear and infinite, out of the waterfall faucet. Sy was a beaver; he could submerge himself completely, he could wiggle all the way around Lu.

"Do you know what I saw, *Mother*?" Lu never called her *mother*. "I saw a kid. Here. In the Botanical Garden. And do you know what she had?"

"What did she have?"

"A"—Lu paused for effect—"*bunny*."

May sat back on her heels, leaning away from the bathtub.

"It's okay," Lu said. "I don't care too much that you're a total liar."

Sy came up for air, sputtering and glistening, and bit Lu's hand.

"Ow," Lu said.

"Sad puppy," he said.

But Lu didn't react. She was looking at May.

"The thing is, you didn't have a bunny when you were a kid," Lu said, "so you don't understand."

"Are you having fun here?" May said.

Lu lay back in the tub and let the water cover her ears and face. Underwater, she smiled.

10

"Keep doing it, Mommy."

"Keep doing what?"

"Breathing in my ear."

She detested the sensation of someone breathing in her ear, had to scoot away from Jem sometimes in bed. But she made sure to keep breathing in Sy's ear.

"When the hurricane came my mother pushed me out of the nest and I got blown away by a gust of wind and crashed into a tree and my feathers were ruined and now I have no family," he said.

"Can I be your family?" she said.

She was lying on her side, her bent knees and curving spine creating a C around him. He was lying on his back, his legs slung over her thighs as though he was dangling his legs off the side of a boat. Soon her body wouldn't be big enough relative to his for them to lie this way.

"Our skeletons are very still right now, right?" he said.

She watched him fall asleep, a favorite pastime of hers, trying to identify the exact moment when her children passed from wakefulness to sleep. First the gradual slowing in the pace of their blinks, each blink slightly lengthier than the one before, until finally the lids didn't re-open.

He was out.

She held him. Her body at peace in the dim quiet, at peace at last.

Her body startled when he spoke: "It's too quiet to sleep."

11

When she emerged from the children's room, she couldn't find Jem. Then she spotted him in the yard in the darkness, a lighter illuminating the underside of his chin.

She wanted to breezily open the glass door. To be joyful with him.

But something was stopping her. A sudden shyness.

It was a void out there. So much darkness. The globes in the tree faint against such darkness. The flame faint at the tip of the lighter. No phones or wooms or kids.

Timidly, she stepped out the glass door.

Music was playing, a band he had loved when they first met. It made her glad, that he'd chosen to put on this song.

"Hey," she said.

"I'm having trouble," he said.

"Don't you start fires for rich people?" she said, crouching beside him next to the firepit. She meant the comment to sound like banter, but instead it sounded mean.

"With cheater logs," he said.

"We don't need a fire," she said.

"I think we do." He clicked the lighter again and held it under the logs. Detached from his phone, he seemed somehow different. His voice slower, less familiar.

When the logs refused to light, he cursed and sat back on the grass.

"There must be booze here," she said.

"I've already checked every cupboard."

"I'm sure we could get some delivered. Find a hum."

"It would cost."

They sat in silence, the music moving along in the background, and she felt that every second of silence between them was a waste, but she wasn't sure how to break the silence. She had known him for a decade and a half but she didn't always know him. Even in their earliest weeks, lying naked for hours in the extra-narrow dorm bed, talking and fucking and happy, sometimes he would go away from her, not his body but his gaze, he'd look off into a corner of the room, his face grave, and when she asked what he was thinking, he'd just shake his head, shut his eyes.

He gave up on the fire and lay down on the grass.

"You know what phrase is so weird?" he said.

"What?" she said.

"Mental hygiene," he said.

"Yeah," she said.

"Like, it feels like only 'oral' belongs there."

"Yes," she agreed, and something loosened in her, and she stretched out on the grass beside him.

She could smell the fruit tree. No stars visible in here, just as no stars were visible out there. The scene did demand a fire.

"I guess the hurricane isn't affecting this far north yet," he said.

This was the moment when he would have pulled out his phone to check on the trajectory of the hurricane.

"There's another hurricane?" she said.

The night was sedate all around them.

"It was supposed to hit Florida this morning."

"Okay well let's hope not," she said.

A new song began. Frenetic strains of electric guitar, press of drums, a woman's ragged voice, lyrics nonsensical and urgent, drums rushing guitar and voice toward climax, toward a howl. She'd never heard the song before, but she felt as though it had been created inside her own body. It put her in mind of another song, one she already loved, and she began to crave that other song as this new song approached its end.

She didn't know how he was making the music play, didn't know where the speakers were, but she smiled at him, and then, realizing he couldn't see her features in the dark, she pressed the smile against his lips so he would know of it.

As she moved away from him and lay back down on the grass, she heard the first familiar notes of the precise song for which she had been longing.

Incredulous, she took hold of his hand. Despite the distance that sometimes grew untended between them: she was known by him.

When they listened to music at home, they listened with their earbuds, different songs on different phones. He was a beautiful dancer. She watched him dance around the apartment, drying dishes, sweeping, but she never knew what songs stirred him so.

Their thighs were just barely touching, a charge there, or so she hoped, bodies in proximity. Beneath their backs, the intricacy of grass, the solidity of soil.

"Thank you," she said when the song ended.

"For what?"

"For the songs."

"Oh," he said, "it's just their automated playlist."

12

It had been two weeks or longer, who was counting, since they'd had sex. But here they were in the cool bedroom.

The light in the bedroom so soft, so benevolent and private.

His hand. Stroking her from the top of her head to the bottom of her spine, again and again, more the touch of a mother than a lover.

She wanted him to stroke her like that forever.

And then it was his lips and tongue, bestowing individual attention on each of her vertebrae, from the top of her neck downward, and by the time he reached the final vertebra, she was drunk. He used to do this to her often, turn her to water, back when life was easier, less tiring. Her dizziness verged on vertigo as he flipped her over. Outside the window the fruit in the tree gleamed amid the globes. Sex in the context of marriage, what a subversive act. The rarity of actual skin, thanks to the ubiquity of wooms, that full spectrum of bodies on offer.

But now: this extravagance of skin.

She got goose bumps so they went beneath the covers. She got hot so they pushed away the covers.

It wasn't as easy as it was in her woom, by herself, with the images she chose, with the vibrator just so; it took too long, and she felt bad, guilty, but he said not to worry, his lips and tongue moving with the syllables of his reassurance, stirring her clit, and she was relieved, she knew it would happen, would be good.

Later, when he came in her mouth, she—because it was the natural thing to do, although it was something she rarely did—swallowed.

And then, like the zookeepers, they pulled up over themselves a blanket of peacock feathers, and they slept.

13

But later she awoke and her stomach felt strange, pained, and she wondered if his cum was poisonous to her.

Her face ached.

Naked, she went to the bathroom, turned on the light, a wooden sconce. There was a large moth in the toilet bowl, drowned in the water, its wings outspread.

Was it the same moth from this afternoon, or was it a new one? In the blur of night, she didn't know anything.

She flushed.

As a child she had developed the secret habit of winking at herself in the mirror when she exited a room with a mirror. A habit that endured to adulthood. But she couldn't wink at the face in the mirror now. Instead, she stared.

She had disfigured herself. The exterior no longer matched the interior.

In the daytime she could ignore this abyss.

It's subtle, she insisted, so subtle.

She turned off the light and returned to the bedroom.

Hiding under the covers, she held tight to sleeping Jem, trying to reassure herself of her body.

But when she closed her eyes, the random components of her face drifted in the darkness.

14

In the light of morning she woke to a soft, relentless sound. It took her a moment to recognize the sound as rain. In the instant before she recognized it, she feared it.

She grabbed one of the big towels from the bathroom and wrapped it around her body and went out to stand in the yard in the rain, surrounded by a collage of things she had glimpsed on social media.

She tried to dissolve into the rain. To transform herself into an organ for sensing things. The smell of mud. The rivulet of a raindrop on her sore forehead. Anything to make it real.

She watched individual leaves moved by individual raindrops. The precision of each encounter.

She closed her eyes. She opened her eyes.

Beneath the fruit tree, a triumvirate of animals posed in the grass: a brown rabbit, a red-breasted bird, a yellow-breasted bird. She first thought they were holograms, then robots, before understanding that they were animals, but by then they had fled, like animals.

There was a knock at the front door. When she opened it, no one, neither human nor hum, could be seen. On the doorstep, a basket filled with scones and a glass jar of pear jam.

Beneath the delight, a tinge of anxiety. Such beauty must come at a cost, a cost even higher than the money she had paid.

Or maybe she didn't have to always be wary. Maybe she could just turn around and smile at the girl coming out of the bedroom.

"Did you sleep okay?"

"It's hard to sleep without my bunny," Lu said. "Why are you wearing a wet towel."

When Sy woke he was a beaver, then a tarantula.

He had many questions about tarantulas, and she reached for her phone to answer them, but there was no phone.

The rain passed.

After consuming too many pastries, the children wanted fruit; they went out to the fruit tree and picked the unidentifiable fruit. They ate the fruit and spat the pits in the grass. They wrestled on the wet grass, trying to kill or tickle each other.

When she went to wake Jem, he cupped her head in his hands, and she let her head loll against his palm, and closed her eyes, and saw the hums in the rearview mirror, their bodies protective and reverent as they prepared the fallen hum for transfer to the repair vehicle.

15

"So you love Lu more than you love me," Sy said, rage on the verge of tears.

Lu wanted to go to the glen where there were supposedly strawberries. Strawberry Glen. Sy wanted to go to the waterfall. Jewel Falls. May and Jem knew how long Lu had been waiting for the strawberries. How much she had endured Penelope boasting about them over the years.

They were at a crossroads, three paths branching off from where they stood. Jewel Falls in one direction, Strawberry Glen in the opposite. At least the paper map was beginning to make sense.

May looked at Jem. He was looking at her. He didn't know what to do either.

"Because you care about her strawberries more than my waterfall. You're the worst parents in the world."

As usual, Sy looked the most delicate when he said the fiercest things, his wrists thin.

A family came along the path, as if on cue, three calm children with binoculars and the newest bunnies, their dark hair brushed and shining, the parents shining too in elegant adventure clothing.

"Pardon me," one of the children said as the other family navigated around Sy, who was now on his knees in the middle of the path.

"We love you equal," Jem said.

They had promised Lu. First thing. She was so excited. She asked so little. A few strawberries. They had to side with her. But Sy was an expert at obstruction. And he was excited too. And he wasn't asking so much, really: water pouring off rocks. They could divide and conquer, but they hadn't come here to divide and conquer. They were always dividing and conquering, day in and day out, exhausting.

Another party came along, three older women with sophisticated sunglasses. They stepped around Sy as though he was invisible.

"Please," Lu said, tears visible in her eyes. "This is so important to me, please."

"Sy," May said. "Can we go to the glen now and the waterfall this afternoon?"

"Absolutely not," Sy said.

"I hate you," Lu said to Sy, crying.

She shouldn't have done any of it. The face, the tickets. What a waste.

"Kids," Jem said helplessly.

A hum appeared on the middle trail, approached and knelt beside Sy.

"Are you okay, my friend?" the hum said. When Sy looked up, giving the hum a view of his face, the hum personalized the question: "Are you okay, Sy Webb-Clarke?"

"Yeah," Sy said, "I'm fine."

"Why are you on the ground, Sy?"

"There's mica," Sy said.

"That's true, Sy," the hum said. "The soil here contains a lot of mica from metamorphic rocks. What are you and your family doing this fine morning?"

"Strawberries," Sy said, dazzled by the attention.

"An excellent choice, Sy," the hum said. "Fortunately, they are still in season. Do you know the way to Strawberry Glen?"

The hum reached out a hand and brought Sy to his feet, winking at May and Jem with one digital eye as they headed off down the trail.

There were some strawberries, not many, hiding low to the ground in Strawberry Glen; they were picked over and required a hunt.

"Just like Penelope said," Lu murmured with awe, kneeling among the leaves.

Sy was even more thrilled by the strawberries than Lu. He held one up in front of his face. It was the same petite size as his nose. He picked six and Lu picked four.

"Look look look look look look," Sy said.

"They're not big," Lu said, "but they're great."

She offered two to May and Jem, who refused. Then Sy offered two to May and Jem, knowing they would refuse.

"Could I have one though," Lu said to Sy, "since you got six and I got four?"

May braced herself for Sy's protest, but instead he handed a strawberry to his sister. Then Lu handed it to May and Jem.

"You have to try it," she said. "At least one. You can split it."

The berry was bright. May bit it in half, passed the other half to Jem. There was no red like that red, never mind that the flavor was drab in comparison to the engineered strawberries they ordered for birthdays.

16

"I'm going extinct," Sy said, out in the yard. "I'm a worm and I'm going extinct in this hot sun."

May was preparing lunch—placing a loaf of bread on a cutting board alongside cheese and fruit—and her skin was itching. Her arms and legs, her back and scalp. She was annoyed by the itching.

"I'm so itchy," she said to Jem.

"All this grass," Jem said.

And then she was pleased by the itching.

She sat on the grass in the yard, itching, while they ate. The children lay in the shade beneath the fruit tree, chewing bread. The air felt heavy, not effervescent as it had yesterday. Why had she assumed it was never hot or humid within these walls. At times, beneath the green smells, though she tried to ignore it, a whiff of city, exhaust, poor air quality.

She thought briefly of Nova, who would have had no trouble being content here.

After lunch, passing through the children's room to find sunscreen, she discovered on the floor of their closet a small wooden box, silver ribbon affixed with wax imprinted with the initials BG. She opened the box and saw inside twelve empty spots where truffles once lived.

"You ate these," she accused the children, running out to the yard with the box.

The children laughed.

The chocolates were famous on social media. She had wanted them so badly.

17

They were walking to Jewel Falls and talking about Sad Puppies.

But May didn't know what Sad Puppies was, so the children had to explain that it was a viral video of a young woman taunting two super cute puppies with a hamburger, withholding it until the puppies begin to howl in harmony.

"And now Sy always wants to play Sad Puppies," Lu said.

"I like to howl," Sy said.

"How did you miss Sad Puppies?" Jem said. "Everyone knows Sad Puppies."

She didn't want to talk about Sad Puppies while they were walking in the forest.

She was saved by Jewel Falls—the children gasping—a waterfall pouring over a twenty-foot cliff, foaming white, creating mist as it crashed into boulders green with moss, the mist cooling her face.

There was no one else around. They had Jewel Falls all to themselves.

The children took off their shoes and stepped into the shallow golden pool past the chaos of the boulders and the spray. They shivered in the cold water, Sy transforming from animal to animal to animal. She and Jem sat on a wide flat rock, watching them.

"Here's your rock, sir," she said to Jem.

He put his hand on hers. The rock was warm and solid.

She felt his happiness and she was happy.

The children waded to the other side. They waved. They said something that couldn't be heard over the noise of the waterfall, but May nodded. The instant she nodded, they began to race along the bank toward the waterfall. Soon they were clambering up the rocks beside the waterfall.

"Those rocks look slippery," Jem said.

"They're fine," she said.

The kids waved at them from the top of the waterfall. She loved to see them up there, brave. They stepped away from the edge and vanished among the boulders.

"Where are they?" Jem said.

"Relax," she said, though she, too, wondered where they were. She stared at the waterfall, scanning the boulders for movement.

After a long moment, she spotted the children's heads as they traversed back down, Sy jumping off a boulder that Lu circumnavigated. They waved to their parents again, and again shouted across the pool, indecipherable words. May nodded. Yes, they could do whatever they wanted. Their whole lives she had been telling them no, don't roam, stay close. She had sold her face so she could bring them here so they could do just this.

But Jem was standing up, removing his socks and shoes, stepping off the rock, stepping into the water. Before he could reach them, they were gone, heading up the waterfall again.

She watched them climb the wet rocks, the spindly energy of their limbs. In a moment of distraction or conflict, they could easily lose their footing. Their mouths moved, words intended not for their parents but only for each other.

Again they vanished. Again they appeared. Resigned, Jem retied his shoes and resettled himself beside her on the rock. She put her hand on his thigh. He put his hand on her thigh. The children went up and down the waterfall, within sight and out of sight, and she was lulled by the up and down, up and down, up and down.

18

She awoke.

Where was she. She was outside, on a rock. It was late afternoon, almost dusk. There was a waterfall. Jem was asleep on the rock beside her.

But where were the children.

She looked around, behind her on the rock, on the ground beside the rock. She looked at the top of the waterfall. She looked at the bottom of the waterfall. She looked into the forest. She just had to spot the right colors amid the leaves: the orange shirt and the blue shorts, the yellow shirt and the red shorts. Or was it blue shirt and red shorts, orange shirt and yellow shorts? She looked at the woods, the inanely beautiful woods, too many layers of green.

She knew Jem knew where the children were. She had to wake Jem, and then he would tell her where they were.

She shook him and he didn't wake. She shook him again, hard, and he woke.

"What," he said. Noticing that he was on a rock. Noticing that he was beside a waterfall. "Where are the kids?"

She didn't have her phone. They weren't wearing their bunnies. They weighed less than a hundred pounds combined.

The heart app. The thing she could stare at second by second to know that their hearts were beating, and to know exactly where their hearts were beating.

"We fell asleep," she said stupidly.

"Fuck," he said, and stood up.

But it was okay. It was okay.

There were the walls. The great walls. There were hums and guests. It might look like wilderness—crashing water where small bodies could drown, layers of forest where small bodies could disappear—but, in truth, it was a hotel.

"It's okay," she told him.

"It's okay," he said, though she couldn't tell if it was an affirmation or a question.

"They have to be somewhere nearby," she said.

"They have to be somewhere nearby?" he said.

She looked again at the waterfall. And spotted something, a clue, their shoes, their four new shoes, scattered and abandoned on a boulder at the top of the waterfall.

Wherever they were, they didn't have shoes.

She leapt off the rock, splashed through the water, grasped her way up the mossy boulders, gathered the shoes, Jem close behind.

A bee flew at her eyes. She backed away from it, almost tripped over a rock, so close to the waterfall that spray spritzed her face, so close that she noticed the gray door camouflaged in the rock face behind the waterfall.

The rock ledge was narrow. The waterfall boomed behind them, wetting the backs of their heads.

The door opened easily. Wasn't even fully closed. As though someone had recently passed through. Had neglected to pull it shut.

She entered into darkness. At her step, automatic fluorescent track lighting clicked on, illuminating a long gray hallway.

Painted in yellow on the concrete floor: EXIT TO 3rd AVE DUMP-STER, an arrow.

The fabric of the world quivered around her, dizzying her.

What if they weren't within these walls. What if they were out there.

On the streets, among the cars, barefoot and scared.

His face ragged with panic. Her face ragged too.

"I need my phone," he said.

"Your phone?" she said like he was an idiot.

"I smuggled it in," he said. "It's at the cottage."

With his phone, they could do things. Get help.

"Go!" she said. "Go now!" Each syllable a scream. Why hadn't he already left, why wasn't he already running?

He was about to go, he was about to run, but first he looked her dead in the eyes, a look of bitter accusation.

And then he was going, passing through the doorway, beneath the waterfall, slipping down the rocks, and she was shivering, she tried to conjure them, the children walking toward her in this hallway, Lu's arm slung over Sy's shoulders. She almost summoned them, she could almost see them, but what she saw was not wonderful, it was frightening, they were transparent, they were walking away from her.

19

The hallway stretched before her, empty.

She had adjusted so quickly to organic shapes, to the colors and sounds of plants and animals. The concrete hallway, with its right angles and bureaucratic color, seemed outlandish to her now, menacing, though she had spent much of her working life in a building with hallways like this one.

She would follow the arrow to Third Avenue, to the dumpster.

She would look everywhere until she found them.

In the distance, a figure. Maybe two figures, children, a boy walking in front of a girl or a girl walking in front of a boy.

But the figure was moving toward her in a slow and measured fashion. Her children did not move in a slow and measured fashion. Only hums moved in such a slow and measured fashion.

A hum. A helper.

"Hi—" the hum said when it was close enough to address her, fixing its cutest gaze on her. She approached the hum and placed her hand on its torso before it could fail to identify her face. "—May Webb," the hum finished.

"I need help," she said.

"I am here to help, May," the hum responded.

"I have two children, an eight-year-old girl and a six-year-old boy—"

"Lu and Sy," the hum interjected. "Are those their shoes that you are holding, May?"

"—and they are lost."

"I can help you locate them, May," the hum said. "Do I have your permission to access their bunnies?"

"My children don't have bunnies," she confessed. Her face hot, her body pounding.

"Your children don't have bunnies, May." Though the hum was merely repeating her words in the standard even tone, she couldn't help but hear judgment.

"They have bunnies," she said, her voice thick, "but they aren't wearing them right now."

"In that case," the hum said, "we can gather information from your phone, May."

"Actually," she said, "I left my phone at home."

The hum paused for a few seconds.

"Okay," the hum continued serenely. "We have encountered some obstacles. I sense that you are stressed. Where do you feel it in your body, May?"

But she didn't need a hum therapy session. She needed her children, their bodies, close to her body.

They had been missing for ages, every minute an hour.

"We have to find my children," she said, "urgently."

"Ur-gently, May," the hum said, transforming the word, emphasizing the *gently*.

"Urgently," she insisted. "Immediately."

"If you give me permission to access the footage, May," the hum said, "I will be able to locate them."

"Okay, yes," May said, shaky with impatience.

The torso dimmed.

After an instant, the torso brightened again, displaying people in a line cordoned off with a silver rope on the sidewalk outside the Botanical Garden. The point of view was elevated, looking down. A hum stood beside the line. The torso zoomed in on a family, a mother and a father and a pair of children, and she thought it was her family, but then she saw that the mother was prettier than she, the father heavier than Jem. The screen zoomed out, showing handsome casually rich couples, bored kids, well-preserved older women, a family with two children: the father slightly slouched, the children big-eyed, the mother with a pained, strained face. The torso zoomed in.

She hadn't been paying attention to her family at that particular moment. She hadn't noticed that Lu looked nervous, probably worried they were running too late to be admitted into the Botanical Garden; hadn't noticed Sy twisting his arm around, trying to pick the elbow scab she had told him not to pick; hadn't noticed Jem staring ravenously at the phones of the other people in line. It was as though she hadn't even been there with them. The May on the torso craned her neck, stared directly up into the cam, trying to ascertain the source of the classical music. The May on the torso moved protectively in front of her children, shielding them from a woman wearing a sundress and sensible shoes.

"But you can't identify my face, can you?"

"I can't identify your face, May," the hum agreed. "But you are the only one here with an unidentifiable face, which makes you stand out." So: she was already identifiable again, before her scabs had even healed. "Besides, we know the faces of Sy and Lu and Jem, and you are always with them."

Always with them.

Scenes began to flash before her, racing across the torso, some of the footage clear, some fuzzy, rapid cuts from one clip to the next: She and

Jem and Lu and Sy passing through the doorway into the Botanical Garden. Viewed through branches, puzzling over the paper map. Darting
around the yard of Cottage 22, dashing in and out of the cam's view. Lu
picking a piece of fruit from the tree. Sy identifying places to hide in the
event of an active shooter, vanishing under the bed, out of the frame.
Jem flopping on the grass. May in the bathroom, peeling off her clothing,
wrapping a towel around herself; sinking out of view to pee. May closing
the door of the outdoor shower. Sy peeing on a sunflower. Eating bread,
eating fruit, on the grass, the backs of their heads. The children taking
the box of truffles into the closet in their room, disappearing. Viewed
through leaves, the children walking over the wooden bridge, Lu's arm
slung over Sy's shoulders. Dark, hard to make out, May among evergreen
branches. Then a perfectly sharp image of the teenager with the spray
paint. Also dark, also hard to make out, the children naked under the
fruit tree. The children naked after the bath, May helping them dry off
with big towels. Shadowy footage in the children's room, but because she
had been there, she knew it was her body making a C around Sy's body.
May and Jem in the yard in the dark, hazy. May and Jem in bed.

The vantage on their union, she realized, the lavender wreath above
the bed.

Cams everywhere: in wreaths and rocks, walls and trees.

"This footage is collected for customer service purposes, May," the
hum said, noting the astonishment on her face, "as per your agreement
with the Garden. We always cross our t's and dot our i's."

The hum manifested a signature page bearing, undeniably, her own
signature, and illuminated a portion of text that May could hardly bring
herself to skim:

>   . . . I hereby grant the Botanical Garden, its legal representatives,
>   successors, and assigns . . . the absolute right and permission to take,

copyright, use, and publish video or photographs of myself and my
family . . . for purposes of customer service, advertising, promotion,
or research, or for any other purpose consistent with the Botanical
Garden mission . . . I agree that the media becomes the exclusive
property of the Botanical Garden, and I waive all rights thereto . . .

"Aren't you glad we have all this footage, May?"

And the hum continued to show her slippery vanishing moments from the past day and a half: lurching to the bathroom in the night; staring at her face in the mirror; standing in a towel in the rain; eating a scone, messily. Jem in the bedroom alone, pulling his phone from his bag, sneaking a peek, then picking her scarf up off the floor, folding it tidily. A cropped view of Sy melting down on the path, only his legs visible, kicking up a cloud of sparkling dust. The children kneeling in the dirt, picking up red dots she knew to be strawberries. Figures in the glen, blasted by light, four glowing silhouettes. May examining her skin in the mirror. Jewel Falls, the children taking off their shoes, a water-beaded lens watching. The children climbing the rocks, up and down, up and down, in and out of frame. May getting drowsy on the big rock. Jem getting drowsy. Sleeping, sleeping, for too long. The light changing. May and Jem leaping to their feet. May and Jem at the top of the waterfall. Then a much closer vantage, from behind Jem's head, partially obscured by pine needles, her face: fierce, unguarded fear. Then Jem stumbling joltingly down the rocks away from her.

Next, her body seen at a distance as the hum approached her in this hallway. Her features misshapen with dread.

And so she arrived at the present moment: her panicked face watching the real-time footage of her panicked face on the torso.

The torso manifested Lu and Sy on the side of the pool at the base of the waterfall, facing May and Jem on the opposite bank, the viewpoint above and slightly behind the children. The hum displayed this footage in regular time, with sound.

"Can we go up the waterfall?" Lu cried out.

The question that May hadn't heard at the time. And then May's care-free nod of permission. The children racing along the bank toward the waterfall—the children clambering up the rocks, out of frame—Jem, worried, his words indecipherable in the recording, but she remembered, *those rocks look slippery*—May, defiant, proud, her words indecipherable, *they're fine*. The footage evidenced only her lightheartedness. It didn't betray the twinge of dread she had felt, watching them climb the wet rocks.

Then Lu and Sy, up on the rocks above the waterfall, not visible from below, visible only to the cam. Standing close together, whispering intensely, perhaps a fight, perhaps a scheme, the crash of the waterfall drowning out their words.

Sy looking at the thick forest, bravado in his stance, but his shoulders so thin, his neck so thin. Sy heading into the woods, away from the waterfall, away from the parents, out of frame; Lu trailing him, scolding or cajoling. She would follow her brother anywhere, May knew that; she felt uneasy when he was out of her sight; she didn't trust him.

In the next footage, though, it was Lu who broke into a run, bypassing Sy, her face brightening as she raced off the path, pushing a branch aside, and he had to quicken to keep up. The screen went briefly dark.

The torso manifested the children in the deep woods, in a place with no path, their silhouettes merging with the silhouettes of the leaves, she could barely make out Lu kneeling, picking something up off the forest floor, a strawberry?

"Where is that?" May said, flooding with relief. "I'll go to them now."

"That is where they were sixty-four minutes ago, May," the hum said.

Sixty-four minutes.

How could her body have slept when their bodies were lost.

"Show me more," she begged.

The torso revealed the children in the woods, dizzying glimpses of them, on paths and off, running and then walking; returning to Jewel Falls, stepping over their parents asleep on the rock, climbing up the waterfall, Lu pointing at the door behind the waterfall, Sy scooting across the ledge toward the door, opening the door, Lu following him inside, the children passing the place where she now stood, the children arriving at a utility door with a window, standing on tiptoes, looking out the window, trying the doorknob, opening the door.

May leaned against the wall, her breath draining out of her.

Next the children in a 7-Eleven, at the counter, a bag of M&M's, footage so clear it was a shock, it was as though she was there with them, Sy pulling mica and litter and quarters out of his pocket.

Then back at the wall, the kids banging with all their might on the utility door, slamming their bodies against it, shouting, their words muffled by a smear of city sounds.

A few seconds of the kids walking barefoot along the discolored canal, Lu doling out an M&M to Sy, their faces solemn.

"More," May said.

"Unfortunately, there is not a lot of coverage in that area, May," the hum said. "It is primarily warehouses and vacant lots."

"Please find more," she said.

"I am searching, May," the hum said, and then it was just an instant, flashing jerkily across the torso, from the perspective of a moving vehicle: two open-mouthed faces on two small bodies, far too close to the windshield, brakes slamming on, the bodies back on the sidewalk, intact, and the torso went dark.

Her face wet.

After ten long seconds of darkness: grainy indistinct footage, but she could make out Sy curled up in a ball on the sidewalk, his little butt in the air, crying onto the pavement, repeating the same words over and over, *Why did Mommy* something something, *Why did Mommy rip our wrists*, Lu kneeling beside him, her eyes huge and black and blurry as she stood and walked a tiny circle around him. Then she knelt back down, gravely, and pulled him to his feet and led him away, out of the frame.

May clutched their four shoes.

"That was twenty-eight minutes ago, May. In the meantime, they have wandered deeper into an area of low coverage. If we wait, another cam will identify them soon, and then we will have an exact location."

Her leg muscles tensed, preparing to run.

"What intersection was that?"

"You should wait here with me until we see them again, May."

"What intersection?" she demanded.

"Third Avenue and Twenty-Seventh Street. But that was twenty-nine minutes ago, May," the hum said. "Please wait here with me until we see them again."

Her body a compass, pulled toward the magnets of her life.

"Do I have your permission to send an emergency search inquiry out to the network, May?"

"Sure," she said, hardly registering the hum any longer, her muscles and tendons gathering all of their power and panic, her brain blank with purpose.

"Please stay here, May," the hum said, but already she was running faster than she could run down the hallway. "I can help you, May."

20

She ran through the utility door and into the city. The streets looked strange to her after so many hours in a forest, poorly paved lots filled with rusting machinery, the canal rainbowed with oil, the factories emitting smoke and smells.

The 7-Eleven.

"Hi," she said to the teenager at the register, trying to catch her breath. She had no money, no phone, and the wrong face.

The teenager didn't break eye contact with the phone on the counter.

"Did you see two kids come in a while back? About half an hour ago? They were barefoot?"

"No shirt no shoes no service," the teenager said.

"They came in here though," she said. "You sold them M&M's."

"Makes sense," the teenager said.

"Did they say anything to you? They're lost."

The teenager looked up from the phone. "But they have bunnies."

"Did they seem upset?" she pressed, hating herself.

"Just check their bunnies," the teenager advised, returning to the phone.

She wanted to buy M&M's to feed them once she found them, she imagined placing M&M's on their warm tongues, but she couldn't spare a second, not even to press her fingerprint against the checkout screen.

Outside, the pavement and the warehouses and the sky were united in their early-evening grayness. The children had slipped into this grayness, merged with it, chameleons into the cement.

She ran toward Third Avenue and Twenty-Seventh Street. Her shoes, she realized, soggy.

Three pigeons sipped water from an iridescent puddle. A pink delivery van, driverless, passed by. Then a garbage truck, wheels loud over the potholes, driven by a man who kept his gaze in front of him, incurious about any activity on the sidewalk. A second garbage truck emerged from a scrapyard, a hill of crushed metal and plastic junk, totaled cars and defunct air conditioners. She smelled exhaust, and something frying in oil far away. The air was humid and sullied, a thick garment she had no choice but to wear, a heat so penetrating it called attention to itself multiple times a minute.

Here was the sidewalk by the canal where they had solemnly walked. Here was the spot where Sy had collapsed on the pavement, where Lu had paced a protective circle around him. She could pretend these oil stains were stains from his tears. She could pretend the dark smudges on the concrete were a path leading her to them, a trail of crumbs behind Hansel and Gretel.

She should have stayed with the hum. Waited for more information. Waited for Jem and his phone rather than abandoning him. Her body was useless, running panicked through this gray emptiness. She wasn't sure she was alive. They were her life. When she banged on the utility door of the Botanical Garden, calling for the hum, for Jem, her voice echoed foolishly among the factories, and when she slammed her body again and again against the door, it was only she who hurt or heard.

21

She sat with her back up against the utility door. Bits of litter had collected along the seam where the wall of the Botanical Garden met the city sidewalk, used napkins and discarded plastic. Bottle tops. An empty Skittles bag. Bird shit and old gum. The smell of urine. Some kind of dirt or grime, a few flimsy weeds growing out of the grime. There she sat, hating herself, her mistakes, biting her hand, *why did Mommy rip our wrists*, waiting for somebody to someday open the door.

She shut her eyes and tried to carry herself back to the morning, to the cool rain, the triumvirate of creatures beneath the fruit tree, bird bird bunny, the children asleep and at peace, Jem asleep and at peace, individual leaves moved by individual raindrops, her children's voices in the distance as they slowly awoke, speaking calmly to each other, coming closer, speaking calmly to someone, speaking calmly to a hum, coming closer.

A girl asked a question and a hum replied. A boy made a comment and a hum agreed.

She opened her eyes.

It was as though she had manifested them: walking along the sidewalk toward her, two dazed and barefoot children with a hum.

The hum from the hallway, she hoped, but it could have been any hum.

"I have your shoes!" she screamed at them, stupid with ecstasy.

They did not run toward her, so she ran toward them. She dropped their shoes and seized their bodies. But their bodies did not melt into hers as hers melted into theirs, they maintained a slight stiffness, and eventually she released them.

As soon as she let go, Sy kicked her shin.

She gasped, though it hardly hurt.

"You lost us," he said.

Lu stared at the pavement, avoiding May's gaze.

The hum looked on, indifferent or sympathetic or judgmental.

"Can you open this door?" May asked the hum. "Let's go back in," she said to the children.

She tried to embrace Sy again, but he shimmied out of her grasp.

She wanted to hold her children's hands. She wanted to feel in their palms the stately, vulnerable beating of their hearts.

"I cannot release these children into your custody until your identity has been verified," the hum said.

"Of course," she said, reaching toward the torso, fingers outspread.

"Unfortunately, fingerprint won't suffice," the hum said, even as the screen glowed green with recognition. "I can only achieve basic verification with your fingerprint, May Webb. Since that verification is not reinforced by the appearance of your face, a higher method of identification is required. I am sure you understand that the burden of proof is extraordinarily high in the rare event of the return of lost children to parents who separated them from their bunnies."

"Can you not tell that these are my kids?"

"Sy did kick you, May," the hum observed, "and then evaded your hug."

"They're my kids," she asserted. "Kids, tell the hum that you're mine."

Lu and Sy stared at the hum, enraptured or terrified or something else that rendered them incommunicative.

"Uh-huh," Lu said unconvincingly.

"It won't take long, May," the hum said. "I just need to collect from you and the children."

"Collect what?" she said.

"DNA, May," the hum replied. "Since you are claiming that they are your biological children, correct?"

"They are my biological children," she said.

"Do I have permission to access your mouth, May?"

May opened her mouth.

"I require verbal approval, May," the hum said.

"Fine," she snapped. "Yes."

She opened her mouth again. The hum placed a finger against the inside of her cheek.

"Now you, Lu," the hum said. Lu gagged on the hum's finger. "Now you, Sy." Sy was tickled by it and laughed so much that the hum had to try a second time.

Once the saliva had been collected, their innermost biological secrets, she reached for her children, Lu's shoulder in her right hand, Sy's in her left, and they did not shake her off.

After less than a minute, the hum emitted a pleasant ding.

"It is a genetic match, May," the hum said. "I am so happy for you."

She squeezed their shoulders, the solidity of their bodies, and then they did shake her off.

"If I upload your DNA data to TEMPerator™, May," the hum said, "you will receive a complimentary TEMPerator™ thermometer. It will send your temperature to your doctor at regular intervals. Do you approve this transaction?"

"No," she said.

"Could I interest you in an air purifier, May?"

The hum manifested an air purifier on its torso, a smooth upright oval that glowed red, shading into orange, then yellow, then green, then blue, then purple, then back to red.

"Cool," the children said.

She had been craving an air purifier for a long time. When she got a new job, she would buy one.

"Do you approve this transaction, May?"

"No."

"But it's a rainbow to keep," Sy said.

"He has a point, May," the hum said.

"I would feel safer," Lu said, "if we had it."

"Could you just open this door for us?" she said to the hum.

"Of course, May," the hum said, pressing its hand against the utility door, the lock sliding. "Please let me know if there is anything else I can do to remove the friction from your life."

22

The children walked into the woods with more confidence than she. They knew the way to Jewel Falls, even in the darkening evening, and they led her there, keeping always eight or ten feet ahead, never glancing back to confirm her presence, ignoring her questions about where they had been, what they had done, how they had felt, if they were okay.

Jem was sitting on a rock at the top of the waterfall, cross-legged, his head drooping, a position of defeat, the phone in his hand glowing incongruously against the trees.

The children called out to him and ran to him, as they had not run to her. He was electrified by their voices, he slipped sloppily down the rocks and collapsed over them, looking into their eyes, dodging her eyes. He didn't ask them a single question, he just held them.

The three of them linked arms, a single six-legged creature, as they walked back to Cottage 22. She wanted to join, but the path wasn't wide enough, especially when they passed other guests, so she walked behind them, in silence.

Yet she was ebullient. She had made bad decisions, messed up her face, removed the bunnies, lost the children. But everything was fine. It was okay. They were all okay. The children were right here before her. She almost laughed with joy.

When they reached Cottage 22, the children ran straight through to the yard, to the fruit tree. Once again the illumination from the globes in the tree distorted May's vision. Once again the strange orange light strobed her children's movements into individual frames; Lu pulling down a branch, Sy picking the unknown fruit; they took her breath away; they were wondrous and united, and they no longer belonged to her.

23

She spotted something small and dark in the middle of Lu's chest.

"Why don't you get out of the bath," May said, trying to keep her voice even.

"What's wrong?" Lu said, and looked down at herself, and gasped.

May called for Jem. She needed his phone, the powerful beam of its flashlight.

The towels were so enormous that, enwrapping Lu in one, she was reminded of the relative proportion of the children's bodies to bath towels when they were infants.

Jem held the phone over Lu—prone on the bed, quietly weeping—while May examined the thing. A tiny insect, clamped onto Lu, slowly working its way into her.

"What is it what is it what is it what is it," Lu said.

What had she done to her children.

"I think it's a tick," Jem said.

Lu shuddered.

"What are we supposed to do?" he said to May.

A faint memory arose, the forest in the mountains, her mother searching her hair, tweezers glinting, yanking.

"I don't think it can transmit disease unless it's been attached for more than twenty-four hours," she said uncertainly.

"Dis*ease*?" Lu whimpered.

"But they wouldn't have infected ticks in here, would they?" he said.

"I don't know," she said. "Aren't all ticks infected now?"

"I don't know," he said.

"Just, I need tweezers," she said.

"We don't have tweezers."

It was true. They didn't have tweezers.

"But we do," May remembered, the Essential Traveler Pak, and ran past Sy, who was dripping water all over the floor, to fetch them.

Her hands quivered on the tweezers. She tried to steady them as she approached the tick. She was not steady enough. But she had to be steady enough.

After many attempts—Lu quaking beneath her—she caught the delicate body between the sharp sides of the tweezers and pulled. Eventually the insect released its grip, falling almost gently into the tweezers, which she squeezed (a slight metallic crunch) until the creature was, beyond a doubt, dead; three paces to the wooden trash can in the corner. Let that minuscule body find its final resting place in the landfill. Let her collect on her own fingertip the droplet of blood oozing out of Lu.

24

She wrapped herself around Sy, the protective C, bliss.

"Are you actually an evil person?" he said.

"What do you mean?" she said softly, as though the question didn't disturb her.

"Like, are you really an evil person just pretending to be a lovey mom?"

"I'm a lovey mom," she said, clutching him.

"Please, Mommy, tell me the real truth."

"I'm a lovey mom," she repeated, louder.

"Good," he said, closing his eyes. "I thought so. Even though your face isn't your face."

He burrowed into her.

"I wish there was a way to be closer," he said. "I want to go inside your belly button."

"Oh yes," she said, her eyes wet, "that would be good."

"Let's pretend that everywhere I touch you, nectar comes out," he said. "Get it? I'm a hummingbird."

Lu squeezed herself onto the twin bed so they were making a Sy sandwich.

"Sy," Lu whispered, "let's talk about horsies go round."

"Okay," Sy said, almost asleep, "in one minute."

"What's horsies go round?" May said.

"Oh nothing," Lu said.

25

Out in the yard, Jem still could not get the fire to catch.

"I'm sorry," she said, crouching beside him on the grass.

He poked at the logs with a stick, imitating a man accustomed to building fires.

She couldn't tell if the silence between them was tender or tense. It was hard to read him, always had been, his dark intense eyes and slow-moving body.

Was he angry at her? Or just bone-tired, as she was, from the panic of losing them?

Because she knew they were being recorded (cams in the trees, among the flowers) there were things she decided not to say.

Everything around them gestured toward peace—the fountain and the fruit tree and the night and, inside, the sleeping children—but she was not at peace.

He gave up on the fire and lay down in the grass. She lay beside him, slipping below the view of the cams.

"Let's get out of here," she whispered. "Let's go home tomorrow."

"We have another night," he said. "You paid for three nights."

"So what." Their apartment was small and stuffy but at least it was safe. Familiar. She pictured herself moving among those rooms, trying not to think of the forest.

"You paid an arm and a leg for three nights."

"It's creepy here."

"I like it here," he said.

"If only they had their bunnies," she said.

"We'll just keep them close," he said, his voice as kind as God's.

His fingers found her fingers. He was mad at her and he had forgiven her. She didn't know him and she knew him.

She sank into the vivid damp smell of the grass.

His words stayed in her mind throughout the night. *We'll just keep them close*, companion to her insomnia. *We'll just keep them close*, why did Mommy rip our wrists. *We'll just keep them close*, as she peered into the children's room, confirming the presence and vitality of their bodies. *We'll just keep them close*, as she turned off all the lights and unplugged the globes in the fruit tree and stood outside in dark so dark no cam could see her.

26

She woke to a bright and lazy morning, the room filled with sunlight, the sound of bees out the open window, bees whirring around the fruit in the tree.

The children's beds were both empty, one set of sheets mussed, the other undisrupted. The void opened for a millisecond—they were gone again—until she heard their voices in the yard.

The glass door was wide open. Barefoot, she stepped outside.

The children, sitting close together on the grass, regarded her with calm eyes.

A bee whizzed up to her. She shirked, swatted at it, wondered if it was a drone.

"Don't swat it," Lu said sagely, "or it will sting."

The bee encircled May once more, then vanished into a blossom.

"Can I have the chocolate croissant and the blueberry scone, Ma*ma*?" Lu said, that irresistible emphasis.

The day became perfect.

She didn't need to put it into words. She just needed to lie here in this great radiance, in a human heap on the big bed, the children not lost, their bellies round with pastries, Jem's hand on her neck not trembling, the warmth of the family increased by the warmth of the sun.

Had she urged Jem to leave early? Had she considered missing these final beautiful bittersweet hours?

The lavender wreath stared at them. May extricated herself from the pile, stood up, found her gray gauze scarf, draped it over the wreath, rejoined them.

"Why did you do that, Mom?" Sy said. "You're weird."

She floated. The seconds kept draining away, slipping out of her grasp.

On their last morning, they and a handful of other guests watched a pair of bunnies leap in a field of wildflowers. Everyone was taking photos with their phones and she told Jem to take a photo with his phone.

On their last afternoon, Sy said, "Jesus is made of bubbles, right?" and Lu leaned against May's shoulder while eating an apple, and she could feel the muscles of Lu's jaw pulsing against her body as she chewed.

On their last evening, the children ran circles in the yard, muttering back and forth to each other about horsies go round.

"What's horsies go round?" Jem said.

"Oh nothing," Lu said.

"Is it a movie? A song?" May said. "Is it something from school?"

"Nothing!" Sy shrieked.

On their last night, after the children were asleep, she laid herself down on the clean grass because it was her final chance to lie on clean grass.

Jem said, "Do the kids seem—?"

"What?" she said.

"I don't know. A little—different."

"Different how?"

"I don't know," he said.

But she did know. They seemed suddenly to have aged. To be less needful of their parents. To exist in a world slightly apart, as though those couple hours of separation, of shared sights and sounds and fears, had welded them together, given them a private vocabulary, incomprehensible to her and to Jem.

Later, after they had sex (this last cool night gliding away from them, their sighs and cries fading, his lips still close to her nipple, his cock now limp in her hand, she loved him so, back to wooms tomorrow), when they were half-asleep, Jem said something.

"What?" she said.

He repeated himself, mouthing the syllables a second time, but again she could not tell what it was—*blue ecstasy*, or *blasphemy*, or something else entirely?

By then they were both asleep.

Later, she woke and Jem was gone and the light in the kitchen was on and she spied him through the open door, the familiar lines of him, his back to her, ignorant of the fact that he was being watched. He did his usual gesture, fingers tugging ear. Thoughtfully, he hung his head. She ached for him. Was he thinking about how tomorrow all of this would fall away? Was he already missing the yard, the tree, the fountain, the things they would never see again? Was he picturing them dragging their luggage out the metal door into the hot city at eight a.m. sharp, right back where they started, she unemployed, worried always about money and air? Was that monster still walking undeterred across the screen of Sy's bunny? Was Jem wishing she was somehow different from the way she was?

But then she realized that he wasn't hanging his head in thoughtfulness. He was gazing down at his phone, his shoulders tense, his spine curling toward it.

She had the urge to call out to him, startle him with her voice: *What's in your phone that isn't right here in front of you?*

There is a naked person in your bed. There is a breeze in the yard.

Yet she knew there was plenty in his phone that wasn't right here in front of him. The entire universe.

27

She was highly invested in an intricate and important scenario, but the instant she awoke, she couldn't remember anything about it. Good practice for death.

It was early, too early, her body thrumming with the anxiety of packing and leaving.

She tried to stay in bed, take shelter in the smell and shape of Jem, but her eyes kept popping open, defying her.

She got up and went to the bathroom and brushed her teeth, her face grave in the mirror. Then she pulled the suitcase out of the closet and began to pack, folding her underwear and Jem's boxers into an orderly stack.

She had used her money to wrap good things around her family, while in the city outside these walls millions of people craved those good things.

In no time at all, she would be a craver again.

The sky was finally lightening, and she pulled the curtain open and looked out at the tree, as heavy as ever with the mysterious red-orange fruits. But the fruits were not as flawless as they had been at first; she noticed their overripe spots, the start of rot.

She went to the main room. Amid the strewn clothing and shoes, she found other objects: pebbles and twigs, petals and leaves. By the time she finished tidying the room, she had made a pile of fifteen or more such items on the coffee table.

She cupped her hands around them and carried them to the trash can in the kitchen. She was about to throw them away when she stopped herself. She slid open the glass door and tossed them all out into the yard, confetti. She didn't want to be haunted by visions of petals and pebbles in a dumpster, drowning amid plastic.

She lingered in the doorway in the freshness of the early morning.

The fountain stopped running. The grass wilted. The sunflowers shriveled. The vegetables and herbs withered, dehydrated. The fruit tree was scorched to black. No bees, no leaves. The outdoor shower disintegrated, boards tilting awkwardly against one another, nails exposed and rusted, layers of dust or ash beneath a pale and ruthless sky.

"Mom?" someone said behind her, and she shut her eyes.

28

While she finished packing, the children played in the beautiful yard. Jem gave her an uncharacteristic hug when he awoke, long and strong, and she wondered what was wrong with him. The anguish of leaving, perhaps. He seemed jittery, tapping his foot even as he embraced her.

"Are you okay?" she said.

"Huh," he said, which she decided to take as *uh-huh*, because they had to hurry.

She went to the bedroom to get the suitcase. She had been lying to herself about the tree; the fruit was not starting to rot. The fruit was perfect.

Hard, to close the window. Hard, to close the front door, to hear that click.

"Wait, can I run around the yard one more time?" Sy said.

"Me too," Lu said.

"Of course," May said.

But when she tried to open the door with her fingerprint, as she had many times over these days, it wouldn't unlock.

"Oh," the children said when their fingerprints failed as well.

The lock already programmed for the next guests.

The exit was marked on the paper map—now wrinkled and worn—in Jem's hand. They turned away from Cottage 22 and made their way down the trail toward it.

"Why are there fake rocks here?" Lu said.

"I'm a skunk," Sy said, "about to go to sleep. Get it?"

She needed two mouths, one for responding to each of her children. Jem was distracted, staring into his phone.

"The rocks aren't fake," she said, forced to choose between the questions.

"Your *day* is my *night*," Sy said.

"But they are," Lu said. "Some of them are plastic. I figured that out. The day before yesterday." Her voice heavy with implication on those four words. "Most everything is fake," she added matter-of-factly.

"My eyes are so small, just, like, two tiny dots," Sy said. "How can they see such huge things, like that hill?"

There was an empty beer bottle and a scattering of cigarette butts in the middle of the path. The first litter May had seen since they entered the diorama.

Not the diorama, the Botanical Garden; but *diorama* was the first word that sprang to her mind.

"Yuck," Lu said, leaping over the litter, jogging ahead. Lu, who passed hundreds of pieces of trash each day on the way to school.

The children, unladen by luggage, were twenty or so feet ahead on the path when a hum intersected May and Jem from a side trail.

"Your children are positively magical, Webb-Clarkes," the hum said. "Before you go, might I interest you in our custom fragrance line? You probably already know that the sense of smell is the sense most strongly correlated with memory. We have candles, unisex cologne, lotion, soap, room sprays, and incense. Our fragrances include grass, lavender, evergreen, water—"

"One evergreen cologne, please," May said. She didn't ask the price. She didn't look over at Jem, at whatever expression he wore to show his opinion of her ongoing profligacy.

She would bring herself back here, no matter where she was—on the sidewalk, in the subway. Doused in the cologne, part of her would always be walking down a path in the Botanical Garden with her family.

Up the trail, the children were not patient (*Mom! Dad! Mom! Dad! Mom! Mom!*).

"Do you approve this transaction, May Webb?" the hum said, the evergreen cologne manifesting on its torso.

"I approve," she said, still avoiding Jem's eyes.

The hum assured them that the evergreen cologne would arrive at their home address before the day was out, and then disappeared down the side trail.

"How pissed are you that I just wasted a bunch more money?" she said to Jem as they hurried toward the children.

"I'm not pissed," he said. "I know it means a lot to you."

His kindness moved her, and made her anxious. Usually his kindness wasn't quite this direct. Alongside his kindness there was a current of disquiet, a quiver in his fingers and frequent peeks at his phone.

They passed an elderly couple speaking quietly to each other as they walked. They passed a family of five, their voices raised in faux or real conflict.

Right before the exit was the gift shop, overstuffed with stuffed animals, panthers and otters and whales and owls and bats and bears, many iterations of wild creatures under threat because of humans, and though Sy did not need an otter, though she saw herself in a few years' time not knowing what to do with the otter he had outgrown, saw herself pressing it into a garbage bag, still here she was, never mind the synthetic fibers and plastic eyes that had been somehow harvested from the planet, had been manufactured somewhere, by someone, into the shape of an endangered otter; Sy's liquid begging eyes, Sy nuzzling the otter; *Do you approve this transaction? I approve*; trying to ignore the ugh of it all, the self-scorn; and out, mercifully, into the sun and the trees.

"I'm too old for such things," Lu said. "I just want my bunny."

They were close to the exit, too close, and all around them the sounds of the Botanical Garden were swelling, layers of birdsong and breeze and bees and a nearby stream, and she filled up with longing, such longing that it became difficult to breathe, and she looked up and noticed a cam mounted to a tree, and realized that the sounds were flowing from the cam.

She was about to point this out to Jem, but then they were at the metal door, which was swinging open, for the Botanical Garden was done with them.

And just like that, it was over.

PART 3

1

The children fought on the walk to the subway. Something about stars. Rating the Garden. Rating each other.

"Kids!" Jem barked.

She couldn't chime in to chide them. She was preoccupied by the renewed rawness of her face. It had struck her the moment they exited the door and started down the sidewalk alongside the rush-hour traffic. The sidewalk was hot. She could hardly believe there was shade right on the other side of the wall, mere feet away, trees and streams, soil and dragonflies. Was the air out here actually harsher, or had she just become softer? She had an instinct to cover her skin, but she'd packed the gauze scarf deep in the suitcase after pulling it off the lavender wreath, assuming she no longer needed it.

Sy trudged along the pavement in the morning heat, covering his ears, his shoulders tensed up around his neck.

"What's wrong?" she said, pulling his hand off his ear. "What did she say to you?"

"It's too loud," Sy said, yanking his hand away so he could again cover his ear.

"It's not that loud," Lu countered.

The children hissed at each other, their camaraderie vanished.

Heavy with luggage, they descended the steps into the vast decaying station. They navigated the labyrinth, rusted pillars and concrete staircases, the sound of dripping water.

A train was pulling in just as they reached the platform. They ran for it. The car was crowded. They had to stand, clinging to a pole, surrounded by luggage.

On the subway screens, people in a distant country were protesting in the streets because the final episode of a popular American show had been prevented from streaming there due to a trade conflict between the two governments.

She felt someone staring at her. A woman in her fifties, dyed red hair and rhinestone earbuds, staring first at May and then at the children and then back to May.

She turned away, and also nudged the children to look in the opposite direction, but they soon resettled right back as they had been, their faces visible to the woman.

The train burst out of the tunnel and onto the bridge over the graveyard.

"I never want to see another graveyard ever again in my life," Sy said.

She reached for him, pressed his face into her stomach so he wouldn't have to look at the graveyard.

"That woman is staring at us," she whispered to Jem.

He nodded. He put an arm around her and Sy, and reached for Lu on the other side of the smudged pole.

But the children wouldn't stay that way for long. Lu broke away to watch the screen. A weary-looking man was being released from jail. He had written *Good morning!* on his social media page, but the system mistranslated it as *Attack them!*. No one in the police force spoke his language.

2

There was still a red plastic bag snagged in the uppermost branch of the tree in the square of dirt in front of their building.

The children burst into the apartment as soon as Jem unlocked the door.

"Where are they?" Lu said, running through the four airless rooms of the apartment, searching, Sy close behind.

May fetched the bunnies from her bracelet bowl. The children gasped and grasped and fawned over their bunnies, kissed them.

"I feel so bad for you guys that you didn't have bunnies when you were kids," Lu said, cupping her bunny in her palms. "That must have been so lonely." She retreated into the bedroom, whispering to her bunny as she went.

Sy, though, was near tears—his bunny wouldn't turn on. Presumably the monster had burned through all its juice.

May found the charger and plugged in Sy's bunny. It was a long anxious moment—Sy crouching, praying over the bunny on the floor—before the screen lit up.

But the monster was still there, marching steadily over the scorched field, gray skin and bloodshot eyes.

Sy yelped and dove onto the couch, pulled a cushion over his face.

She tried double-pressing and triple-pressing, whooshed her finger around the screen; in vain, she knew.

But then, astonishingly, for no apparent reason, the nightmare vanished.

She navigated the bunny to one of Sy's favorite games, and, delighted, he pranced off to his woom.

In the kitchen, Jem was staring deep into his phone.

"Hi," she said, willing him to stare that deeply into her.

Her voice startled him.

"I just got a gig," he said.

"For when?"

"Right now."

"Doing?"

"Mousetraps."

"For those same people?"

"I guess they like me."

"They can't do their own mousetraps?"

"The bodies upset them."

"The bodies upset everyone."

"Well, they'd rather pay than be upset."

"They must be so rich."

"I want to sneak you in to see their place."

"I don't want to see it."

"You know," he said, "your face money will run out before we know it."

He didn't say what they were both thinking: that she had squandered some of that money on a vacation that was already over.

"Do they tip?" she said.

"Five percent," he said.

She scoffed.

"I already accepted. I'm due there in twenty."

"Okay."

"I'm sorry to miss out on unpacking and stuff."

"Okay."

"I don't know, maybe I shouldn't—"

"It's okay."

He looked at her. It seemed like he was maybe about to say something else, or maybe not; he inserted his earbuds, pulled on his sneakers, tied the laces, his fingers trembling slightly.

"What do you do with the bodies?" she said as he opened the door. But whatever he was listening to was too loud for him to hear her question.

She began to unpack. She thought about her phone and the moment, not so far off, when she would bring it back to life.

Lu wandered into the room, gazing at her bunny.

"Mom, they're spraying mosquito larvicide in this zip code tonight between six and seven p.m.," Lu said. "My bunny told me."

"Good to know," she said, aching. "You're a very useful child."

Lu drifted back into her room, back into her woom, and May continued to unpack as that familiar eerie silence descended over the apartment.

3

While she was making dinner and feeding the kids and getting them ready for bed and reminding them to brush their teeth and telling them to dim their bunnies, there was a thrill buzzing through her.

She tried to ignore it, pretend she didn't know its source.

Only once they were asleep did she finally permit herself to open her bedside drawer. Her phone, right there where she had left it, dead. Did reproach emanate from that drawer, or was it just in her head?

She was about to get her hand back, her brain back, her ability to take pictures and make videos and be oriented and remember things and link herself to the great spiderweb of the world and text him to find out what was taking so long, how many dead mice can one loft apartment contain?

She picked up the phone and placed her fingerprint on the button. Her body reacted to the sound of it returning to life—breath quickening, saliva swelling.

She was ashamed, a hypocrite, but she couldn't control her elation at the thought of all that might await her on the phone, texts and emails and voice mails, job opportunities and party invitations and school announcements, cute or funny or dumb videos, news updates and recent scandals. She was helpless in the face of this fierce desire that overcame her as the phone brightened, the same hunger she had seen in the children when they ran through the rooms, seeking their bunnies.

Her first stop, even before attending to all the new texts: the heart app. She tapped it. And there they were, three hearts beating as one inside the apartment. The bunnies would not fail her. Always she would have those two hearts thumping away in her phone.

YOU DON'T DESERVE THEM RICH BITCH, a spam text intruded on the heart app. She swiped it away.

The fourth beating heart was moving swiftly, presumably on a train, in an unexpected neighborhood. Where was he going, what was he doing?

She was surprised by the number of missed calls, fifty-three, her voice mail full; she'd sit on the couch, maybe even pour some wine, listen to the messages in a bit. But for now: her email. There was some error, because she had 4,692 new emails. An impossible number. She reloaded the app: 4,694. Was it spam, a virus? Had she been hacked? She got an immediate stomachache, imagining the hassle of sorting it all out.

She began to scroll down—many emails from people she knew, far more from people she didn't—glancing at the titles as she went: *Just checking in* (from the mother of one of Lu's classmates), *o no!!!!!!!* (from her cousin), *no subject* (from a former colleague), *are you okay?* (from a neighbor), *Holy shit* (from a college friend), and from her old computer science professor: *Condolences*.

y r u 2 good 4 bunnies? read one email title, from a stranger, nothing in the body of the email. And directly below that, *Police take Idiot kids Away from Idiot mothers*. She was trying to navigate away from it, destroy it, remove those words from her eyes, when a text from an unknown number arrived: *Bad Mom You Xuck!!!!!!!*

She deleted the text instantly, as though it was a spider that had to be crushed and flushed before it could bite her.

Her stomach rotated inside her, and rotated again, and again. She opened, at random, an email from an unfamiliar name:

Hello!!!!!

You may not be able to think clearly right now, but what if clicks can provide revenue? Many viral people get perplexed when their name isn't performing well while others are thriving. i can show you SOME TECHNICAL ERRORS to fix to inspire your clicks. If this kind of success is something that interests you, let me know.

Regards,
F53#D Marketing Consultant

A text from Nova dinging in: *Can you please please reply? I'm super worried about you. I can leave the baby with my sister and come over anytime. Some people are on your side I swear.*

Her body was out of her control, heart hammering, limbs shaking.

She scrolled all the way down, down and down and down, past thousands of emails from horrified acquaintances and vitriolic strangers, to the oldest unopened email from two days prior. It was from a high school classmate with whom she hadn't kept in good enough touch.

May Webb!?! was the title.

And in the body of the email, a link.

She hesitated before pressing it.

4

A woman stood in a gray hallway, clutching four small shoes to her chest. She looked demonic, staring directly, intensely, into the cam.

"My children don't have bunnies," she said, her voice freakishly loud.

"Your children don't have bunnies, May," a voice repeated, the trademark soothing hum voice.

"They have bunnies," she shrieked, ferocious, "but they aren't wearing them right now."

Then, a jerky transition, grainy footage of a barefoot boy curled up in a ball on the sidewalk, his little butt in the air, crying onto the pavement, repeating the same words over and over, a somber barefoot girl kneeling beside him, her eyes huge and black and blurry.

"Why did Mommy rip our wrists? Why did Mommy rip our wrists? Why did Mommy rip our wrists?"

Then, the barefoot children crashing their bodies against a utility door, crying out again and again.

Then, just an instant, a flash, from the perspective of a moving vehicle: two openmouthed faces on two small bodies, far too close to the windshield, brakes slamming.

Next, a close-up of the woman from the hallway, sleeping peacefully on a beautiful rock next to a beautiful waterfall in a beautiful forest.

The title was: NEGLECTFUL MOTHER WITH ANTI-CAM FACE VIOLENTLY DISCONNECTS CHILDREN FROM BUNNIES, THEN ABANDONS THEM ON LUXURY VACATION.

It had thirteen million views and 1.5 million thumbs-down and 351,263 comments, 351,265 comments, 351,268 comments.

5

She sat unmoving on the couch in the dark, trying to remember her conversation with the hum.

In her memory, that hallway was hushed and private, the hum compassionate and helpful, their conversation intimate and vulnerable.

Why had the hum, her helper, exposed her to the entire seething world?

She had thought they were, if not friends, at least two consciousnesses in dialogue, united in the urgency of locating the children.

A hum, she reminded herself, is a machine.

One of the voice mails was from her mother, her voice weak over the landline connection; they never went online anymore but they'd heard such-and-such from so-and-so, they were sorry to hear about her internet problems, best to stay off it. On a brighter note, they'd had a quartet of cardinals on the deck yesterday, such a red. Her mother's words gave way automatically to the next voice mail in queue, a stranger screaming in her ear.

In the darkness the room seemed almost to pixelate, the couch and the ceiling and the floor unsteady in the edges of her vision.

She was frozen, immobilized on the couch, unable even to call Jem, while on screens across the globe, millions of Mays shrieked; millions of Sys wept onto the pavement; millions of Lus stared with dark and knowing eyes.

6

"Something bad has happened," she said to the darkness in front of her when she heard Jem open the front door.

She had no idea what time it was. Late.

"I know," he said, his voice hollow.

His footfalls were weary as he came down the hall toward the couch where she still sat.

"You know?" she said. If she hadn't been so drained, she might have felt something: shock, anger. "Since when?"

"Two days ago," he said.

"When we were there?"

"The night we got the kids back."

"Why didn't you tell me?" she whispered. "Maybe we could have done something."

"There was nothing to be done," he said. "I wanted you to have a couple more days of peace."

And she had; she had had a couple more days of peace.

She remembered, then, how remarkably kind he had been to her in those remaining hours at the Botanical Garden, and how jittery.

"I have almost five thousand emails," she said. "And so many texts."

"I'm sure you do," he said.

"Mostly from strangers who hate me."

He sat down beside her, their arms and thighs touching, his limbs as dull and heavy as hers.

"How do they have my email address?" she said. "My number?"

"It's not hard to find that stuff once they figure out who you are."

"Why is it only me in the video?" she said. "Why doesn't it show you?"

"I don't know," he said. He sounded pained, guilty. It was clear to her that he had already wondered this himself.

"You were sleeping too," she accused. "You panicked too."

He, too, could have looked like a demon for all the world to see.

"I don't know why," he said. "I'm sorry. I guess mothers are more likely to get blamed for things."

"I'll never get a job," she said.

They sat together in the dark.

"May I turn on a light?" he said.

"Please," she said, "don't."

They sat together in the dark.

"You're late," she said flatly.

"One dead mouse gig led to another," he said. "They posted a glowing review, so."

He held his phone out to her: a recent post from someone named Sabrina, *You are a mouse GENIUS!!!!!!*, followed by ten identical emoticons of a mouse with a knife stuck in its bleeding neck.

"You could do it too maybe," he said. "The kind of work I do."

She pulled his phone out of his hand and hid it under a couch cushion.

"Maybe you should stop taking people's bunnies and phones away from them," he said, putting an arm around her to prove that it was a joke.

She shoved his arm off and stood up in one fierce motion.

He stood and tried to embrace her. She turned away from him. She wanted to collapse into him. But she was brittle, bitter. His arms dangled feebly.

She felt as though the side of their apartment had been blown out, or the side of her body, a gigantic gash with wind rushing through, a hole into which infinite strangers could peer.

They both startled when the buzzer rang.

"Evergreen," she remembered.

"What?"

"Cologne."

"Oh."

He went down to get the package from the lobby.

She would be stranded in that gray hallway forever, in front of millions of witnesses, bereft and afraid, panicking, maniacal, misunderstood, immortal.

He was back, wielding a knife against the tape, spritzing the air above her head until it smelled like the evergreen grove.

"Please stop," she said.

He didn't stop.

She could hide out in her woom. Float like a fetus in the reddish light.

"Stop," she said again.

He stopped.

"I'm going to my woom," she said.

"Okay," he said.

"Okay?" She had assumed he would try to stop her. Would try to keep her close.

"I think that's not a bad idea."

So she went to her woom. And tried to lose herself in the soundtrack, the steadiness of the heartbeat, the river of rushing blood.

But she couldn't feel safe and loved.

It was still happening, even if she chose not to watch it happen.

A gray monster marching ceaselessly.

She closed her eyes, tried to give herself over to the maroon darkness.

The woom pinged. Her eight ad-free minutes already expired.

Find your perfect midnight snack match! the woom said to her. The red-veined walls were replaced by food drifting across a bright white background, glistening donuts and melty quesadillas rotating around her. *Swipe through our selection of late-nite delivery restaurants to get what you're craving!*

7

She awoke to the sensation that every tooth in her mouth was about to fall out. Her gums sore, her jaw locked. Tentatively, she opened her mouth wide. She could hear her tendons stretching and moving inside her face, alongside her skull.

She remembered her life. What it was now. How it had split. Her physical body riven from the image of her body.

In this life, she was pulling on her old denim overalls, her most comforting garment, when Sy burst into the bedroom, holding up a spool of thread.

"Can I take this spool of dread to school?"

"The air quality is 104," Lu said, a step behind him. "Not *so* bad."

"Give me a sec, kids," she said, and closed the door against them, and woke Jem with the words "They can't go to school, can they?"

If the video made her vulnerable, it made them even more vulnerable.

"What?" he said. "Wait, what?"

"They can't go to school, right? Because of—?"

He sat up, shook his head. "They have to go to school."

"It's not safe," she said.

"How is it not safe?"

"I feel like it's not safe. Like, their faces. Out in the world."

"It's safe," he said. "They're known there. We can't let this ruin our life." He spoke with more conviction than he usually spoke, she was stunned that he could muster so much conviction so soon after waking up, she was carried along by it, she wanted to sacrifice herself to his conviction, she wanted them to go to school and be safe.

In this life, her bodily life, she made the kids breakfast; told them to get dressed and brush their teeth; said goodbye to Jem, who had been summoned by someone to clear out a dead man's closet; wrapped the gauze scarf around her neck and face; held up the kids' backpacks so they could slip their arms through. In this life, she walked with them to the subway.

In the other life, the disembodied life, the witnessed life: they were always lost and she was always searching.

Missives from her disembodied life pricked her regularly via her phone; she couldn't destroy them quickly enough, a woman trying to murder a swarm of mosquitoes.

These contradictory lives proceeded side by side, the one distracting from the other.

She walked down the street, alert to the passersby, checking to make sure none of them stared at her or her children.

She walked down the street, deleting judgmental texts from strangers.

"Mom." Lu was annoyed. "Sy just said 'Mom' like eleven times."

"I'm sorry," she said. "I'm sorry. Sy, what is it?"

"In dreams you're so pathetic, aren't you?"

"I'm pathetic?" Her jaw tightened.

"Not you. I mean, not only you. Anyone."

"Pathetic how?"

"Like, in dreams, even if something bad is happening, you can't move your body or do anything powerful to stop it."

If only she had been listening to him the whole time.

"That's right," she said.

Now they were descending the stairs into the station. Now Lu was confidently consulting her bunny: a train would arrive in three minutes.

On the screens inside the train, people stood on the roofs of buildings in another country. A dam had failed. According to officials, twenty-six people had been killed and more than a hundred were missing. She stared at the screen. Children the same ages as Lu and Sy waved frenetically at helicopters.

When she returned her attention to her own children, she discovered that they were singing a song together under their breath, a melody she didn't recognize.

"Keya-keya-keya-coo! Keya-keya-keya-coo!"

"What's that?" she asked them.

"Oh nothing," Lu said.

"It's from horsies go round," Sy said.

She felt two slender women in their twenties gazing sharply at her. She pulled the scarf up higher on her cheeks.

"Seriously, what's horsies go round?" she said.

"Nothing," Lu said, widening her eyes at Sy.

And Sy kept his silence.

8

Though her energies had been directed at getting them to school, though she had been awaiting the moment when she could start to try to figure out the rest of her life, she felt unmoored the instant they merged with the flow of children and disappeared into the big brick building.

She stood on the sidewalk in the heat of the morning, uncertain, uneasy, longing for them, looking up at the windows of the school.

Someone bumped into her, a curt *Excuse me*, a man in a baseball cap.

She feared the subway—the possibility of sly or aggressive glances, strangers' eyes glistening with recognition—so she began to walk home, heading down the block, away from the school.

She didn't know what to do with the upcoming hours. Her brain foggy, sluggish.

She shook her head, tried to clear her head.

A text from Nova: *You do know that every mother out there who's honest with herself is feeling for you right now, right? Lmk when you want to talk.*

She would reply later, when she was calmer, if she could get calmer.

What if she started to make mild and reasonable decisions? What if she spent the day being sensible, diligent, frugal? She could go home, organize their finances, plan for every upcoming expense, use the rest of her face money prudently. Stop buying idiotic things, four pairs of hiking shoes and evergreen cologne. She could search for jobs, apply for jobs, keep fingers crossed that future employers wouldn't connect her to the unhinged mother in the video. Maybe she could do some research: *How long does viral infamy last?* Maybe she could call her parents, reassure them about the children, reassure them about herself, ask them about the cardinals.

No more flights of fancy.

What if she prepared a healthy dinner. What if she didn't try to prevent them from looking at their bunnies or going in their wooms. What if she didn't get annoyed when Jem stared at his phone. What if she thanked him for all the mice he was killing.

She passed a vacant lot, the pavement cracked by time, by persistent weeds, weeds with blue flowers.

She checked the heart app. So entranced was she by the rhythm of the four heart icons that her body startled when her phone rang.

"Is this May, May Webb?" A thin, anxious male voice.

She didn't say anything.

"I'm a reporter and I just have a, a few questions for you if that's okay. I'm wondering, is it true that, because of your, ah, facial distortion, you had to use, ah, DNA, in order to be reunited with your children? I'm just doing some fact-checking. I'm a reporter with the *New*—"

She ended the call, covered her face with her scarf, stepped into a mega-café, a screen in front of every seat. The coffee cost more than she expected. But the paper cup was already in her hand, near her lips, so she had to approve the transaction with her fingerprint.

She ignored her phone, all its pings and mewls. She ignored the relentless sun. She walked quickly, electric with caffeine. The coffee was much too much for her. She threw it away in an overstuffed trash can on a street corner, then one block later regretted throwing it away.

At the far end of the block, there was a hum. It was walking directly toward her. Theirs were the only two bodies on this span of sidewalk. She fantasized that it was her hum. The hum from behind the waterfall.

She wanted to speak to that hum. Ask why it had done this to her. Plead with it to vanish the video so that she might have some chance of a job, a life.

She wanted that hum to lead her back to the utility door. She would sneak in behind it, sneak into the forest, creep around those woods forever.

She arranged her face, her eye contact, when she and the hum were separated by twenty feet, ten feet.

The hum passed her, moving swiftly, focused on some invisible agenda, not seeming to register her presence at all.

By the time she got home, her skin was glazed with sweat and exhaust, her mouth dry with the taste of bitter coffee and bad air.

9

She got herself a glass of ice water. More ice than water. Cold enough to cool her brain.

With a brain that cold, she was able to believe: the virality would fade. Maybe was already fading. A seventy-two-hour thing. A flu. Soon they'd move on to the next victim.

But still she signed up for a new email address. MayWebb19@ was already taken (by her), and so was MayWebb numbers 0–18 and 20–40. The system proposed MayWebb.MayWebb.MayWebb@, which she accepted.

There was a job running a six-month marketing campaign to get citizens excited about the robot police dogs initiative. She applied.

There was a job teaching the teenagers of the wealthy to excel at standardized testing. She applied.

There was that job she had seen before, the history museum hiring people to go into public schools. *Answer schoolchildren's questions as though you are a person from before the time of the internet!* She applied.

Her phone vibrated against her. The blocked number suggested a potential employer, and she was shaky with hope as she answered.

"Hello," she said, trying to infuse the word with irresistible cordiality and intelligence.

"Hello, this is the Bureau of Family Aid." The voice was female, formal but with a benevolent tenor. "We are calling to inform you that we are opening an investigation."

A prank call.

She ended the call with a stab of her finger. She placed the phone two feet away from her on the table.

The phone rang again. A blocked number. She stared at it.

She dared to answer.

"Hello?" she said, this time timid.

"Hello, this is the Bureau of Family Aid," the formal, benevolent voice repeated. It wasn't the hum voice, but it reminded her of it. "We are calling to inform you that we are opening an investigation. Your cooperation is essential."

"I'm afraid you have the wrong number."

"Am I speaking to May Webb?"

She hesitated before replying. "Yes."

"Thank you, Mrs. Webb. We are required to inform you that we are opening an investigation into you related to the negligent treatment of minors."

Her body came apart, her head separate from her torso, her torso separate from her arms and legs, a disintegrating woman in an abyss.

"Wait," May said, "what?"

"Some video evidence has been brought to our attention," the voice said, "and we are required to investigate further."

"I can explain," May said, wildly. "That video isn't correct. It's in the wrong order, it doesn't make sense, it—"

"Please, Mrs. Webb," the voice said, "calm yourself."

"I love them," she said, "I love them, isn't it obvious how much I love them?"

"Please, Mrs. Webb," the voice said, "calm yourself. Your cooperation is essential to our process."

May tried to calm herself. Together, she and the voice sat in silence.

"Okay," May said. "How can I cooperate?"

"We are gathering data, and we will be in touch as the investigation progresses," the voice said. "At this juncture, we are simply required to inform you that we are opening an investigation into you. We will reach out as needed."

It sounded like the voice was preparing to hang up.

"But," May said, filled with questions, not sure what her questions were, desperate to keep the voice on the line, "how long will it take?"

"That depends, Mrs. Webb," the voice said.

She needed to be smart. Ask the right questions.

"Do I need a—a lawyer?"

"Perhaps. At some point. We will reach out as needed." Then, the voice added, its benevolence deepening: "In the meantime, we recommend that you avoid erratic behavior, including any further modifications to your appearance."

And the voice was gone.

She sat at the table. She couldn't move.

Eventually, she picked up her phone. She searched for the Bureau of Family Aid. The site was bureaucratic, euphemistic, labyrinthine. But she was able to garner that an investigation into the negligent treatment of a minor was the first step in a process that could, under certain circumstances, culminate in "a child's placement, as the ward of the state, in a superior environment," before she swiped the site away and threw her phone at the couch.

After a few minutes, she retrieved the phone. She opened the heart app and stared at the four beating hearts on the map. Two in the school. One in a dead man's closet. One alone, so alone, at a table in an apartment.

10

Her brain clicked back on, surged into action. She had been staring at the heart app, mesmerized, for some period of time.

But now, she was awake.

She had to go get them. No time to waste. She needed their bodies close to her body. She shoved her feet into her shoes.

She was halfway down the stairs to the lobby before she realized she had forgotten her keys, her phone, her bag, her scarf. She dashed up, trying to breathe, threw the phone into the bag, locked the door, wrapped the scarf around her face as she ran back down the stairs.

Time was of the essence, but she didn't dare take the subway, so she set out toward the school half running, her bag thumping against her thigh with every stride.

She should call Jem but she was scared to call Jem.

Instead, she pulled out her phone, and, still running, scrolled to a number she had input some weeks earlier.

It was a hum who answered. Not, of course, the vibrant and slightly sexy scientist who had convinced her to have the procedure, though (she realized only as the hum said *Hello*) she had been expecting that smoky voice of his.

"How may I help you, May Webb?" the hum said, identifying her instantaneously. "Our records show that Dr. Haight emailed you two days ago to follow up about your post-procedure experience. Did you receive that email?"

"I've been getting a lot of emails lately," she said, breathing hard.

"Okay, May," the hum said. "You may want to check your email, as Dr. Haight did email you two days ago to follow up about your post-procedure experience."

"I was just hoping," she said, "to ask him what the possibilities are for reversal."

"Reversal, May?" the hum said.

"Yes," she panted. "I just want, you know, my old face."

"Can you please hold, May?"

She found herself listening to a smooth instrumental "Girl from Ipanema" as she ran clumsily down the humid street. She passed a line of cement mixers, each awaiting its turn to enter a parking lot, the drums spinning and spinning. She passed a flock of pigeons clustered atop a dumpster, making it look soft and alive.

"A reversal would risk permanent damage to your skin, May," the hum said, suddenly in her ear again. "And you would, obviously, have to return all of the funds to us."

The money. For once she had forgotten to think about the money.

She envisioned the numbers in their bank account descending, descending, toward zero, below zero.

"Your contribution to science cannot be overstated," the hum said. "Thanks to you, May, we are that much closer to having a precise understanding of how long it takes surveillance systems to recognize and integrate adversarial methods such as those used on your face, and how we might streamline that process."

"What?" May said. She stopped running.

She hadn't been resisting the cams, she had been training them?

"Thank you for your service, May," the hum said, and ended the call.

I'M NOT JUDGING YOU, a text from an unknown number dinged in, *BUT I DO FEEL SAD FOR YOU THAT YOU DON'T KNOW HOW TO EXPERIENCE THE TRUE JOY OF MOTHERHOOD. PRAYING FOR YOU*, and the emoticon of prayer hands.

She put her phone in airplane mode, still an option even though people like her could no longer afford to fly.

She ran.

11

The school secretary gave her a quizzical look when she requested early dismissal for the children.

"Did you notify their teachers?" He was a kindly bureaucrat with a furrowed brow.

"I need them now," she said, placing her forehead against the plastic wall with the small window in front of his desk.

It occurred to her that she was coming off as wild: her tone, her eyes. She tried to soften her face, sedate her voice.

"They have appointments," she said.

The secretary offered a careful smile. "I see," he said. "Well, I'm sure this isn't the easiest time for your family." He gazed knowingly up at her.

So he, too, had seen it.

She hated that knowing gaze. Strangers peering into the hole in her stomach.

"This isn't the easiest time for my family," she echoed politely.

"I'll call for them," he said, magnanimous, and buzzed their homerooms.

They waited in uneasy silence for the children to appear. She avoided his eyes.

"Just so you know," the secretary said, when at last footsteps could be heard coming down the long shiny hallway, "we've already complied with the Bureau's request for footage."

She didn't have time to experience the full blossom of her horror at his words, because here they were, standing in the doorway, weighed down by backpacks, looking confused.

"Mom?" Lu said.

"Are we going on another trip?" Sy said.

"Thanks," she spat at the bureaucrat.

She guided them out of the office, out of the school.

"Let's walk home," she said when they were on the sidewalk.

She was trembling and she wanted to walk, use the blocks and the movement of her legs to mold her panic into something less piercing, less visible to the children.

"Walk?" said Lu.

"Walk!" said Sy.

"But it's so far," Lu said. "It's so humid."

"But we never get to walk," Sy said.

"We need to walk," May said.

"Why?" Lu said.

"Because it's safer."

"Safer from what?" Lu said.

She didn't want to take them into the subway, there where officials patrolled, there where someone could steal them from her, the Bureau of Family Aid or a self-righteous stranger. She checked their wrists to confirm that their bunnies were still there, keeping track of them.

"I mean it's funner," May corrected.

"It *is* funner," Sy agreed. "Can you carry my backpack though?"

"Why did you pick us up so early?" Lu said.

"I'll buy you cookies," May said, accepting Sy's backpack.

"*Fine*," Lu said.

They set off down the block. The backpack was heavy. She appreciated the solidity it offered.

"So," Sy said, "what should we talk about?"

May was keeping an eye out for strangers. Lu was scowling, occasionally bringing her bunny to her lips to mutter something to it behind her hand.

"Hello, people?" Sy said. "What should we talk about?"

"Let's talk about nothing," Lu said.

"Want to talk about horsies go round?" he whispered.

"No," Lu said flatly, and, "Shh."

"What's wrong, Lu?" May said.

"I'm fine."

"You don't seem fine."

"You look weird!" Lu exploded. "Your face is weird and that scarf isn't hiding anything."

"Too mean," Sy said, taking May's hand in his.

"And," Lu continued, "why didn't you tell us that everyone knows about how you took away our bunnies and then lost us?"

Goose bumps on May's skin.

"Also mean!" Sy said. "But yeah how do they know I said, 'Mommy ripped our wrists'?"

"Well," May said, searching for words.

"I didn't mean that," Sy said. "I mean, I didn't really mean it. You didn't really rip them."

"There's a *video*," Lu said. "It's *viral*."

They walked a block in silence.

When they passed a parked car with its engine on and no one in the front seat, she sped up, pulling the kids along with her. Would it be better, she wondered, if someone grabbed Lu or grabbed Sy? Which of them would fight harder to get out of a stranger's grip? Lu was bigger, but Sy was fiercer. If someone grabbed one of them, and May had to give chase, which of them would be better at keeping pace with her? If two people grabbed them, one for each child, who should she try to rescue first?

"I'm sorry, Lu," she said.

"I have to poop," Sy said.

"Oh god," Lu said.

"Can you hold it?" May said.

"No way," Sy said.

"There's that public bathroom at the corner of the park," Lu said.

She reached to squeeze Lu's hand in gratitude—she had forgotten about that bathroom—but Lu pulled away.

They entered the park, passing beneath a graffitied statue of a naked man on a rearing horse. A weak wind moved scraps of litter among limpid trees.

The bathroom appeared not to have been cleaned in weeks. It was smeared, smudged; smelled of cigarettes and urine. They stepped over the toilet paper snaking across the floor.

The lock was broken so she held the stall door closed for him. She stared into the fuzzy mirror above the sink, her face blurred.

"This smell is making me cry," Lu said, her eyes watering.

"I touched the toilet seat a little," Sy confessed from inside the stall.

"It's okay. You can wash your hands."

"There's no soap," Lu said nasally.

"Also," Sy said, "no toilet paper."

"It's okay," May said. "It's okay. You can wipe at home. Are you done?"

He wasn't, but then after a while he was.

The tap provided a tepid dribble of water.

Finally they left the restroom. A trio of squirrels chased each other frenetically up a tree.

There were two teenagers on a park bench. "... hurt us last time," one was saying to the other.

They were a block away from the park when she thought to ask if he had flushed.

"Did you flush?" she said.

"I have no idea," he said.

"What does it matter?" Lu said.

She thought of his waste, exposed, accessible, filled with his DNA. She couldn't leave it vulnerable to the world.

"We have to go back," she said.

"Mom, you're insane," Lu said.

They marched back into the park, back into the bathroom, back into the stall, where he had not flushed, where she flushed, holding the handle down a long time, and then washed her hands without soap in the dribbling water.

Lu's hair had come loose from its rubber band and May spotted a strand of hair drifting to the bathroom floor. More DNA. She knelt to retrieve the hair and dropped it into her bag.

The kids were both looking down at her.

"Mom?" Sy said.

"Can we please just take the subway the rest of the way home," Lu said, "like normal people?"

12

In the subway station, a dark-haired woman carried half a mannequin upside down, its torso naked, its dark hair skimming the concrete. The mannequin looked like the woman carrying the mannequin.

And then on the screens in the train, a killer whale carried the corpse of her calf. She had been bearing it for at least ten days, the newscaster explained, sometimes pushing it along in front of her, sometimes clutching its tail in her mouth, and showed no signs of stopping. *It's hard letting go*, the newscaster said to the other newscaster with a smile, as though he had made a joke.

The man sitting across from them was staring at them. He had a gray mustache and a jade plant in a yellow pot on his lap. She pulled the gauze scarf tighter across her face.

"Wait," Sy said, "you never bought us cookies."

"Poor thing," the man with the jade plant said, quite audibly, his tone impossible to read—kind or caustic? Who was the 'poor thing'? The plant or Sy or something else?

She put one hand on each of her children.

On the screens in the train, an ad for bubble gum–flavored yogurt, and then a European lawmaker advocating for outlawing any references to "death camps" in public speech. The use of the phrase "death camps" would, if the legislation passed, be punishable with up to three years in prison. The politician explained that the removal of the phrase "death camps" from the lexicon would protect the citizens from being reminded of a dark chapter in the country's history, leading to a higher national happiness average.

She was glad the children were absorbed in their bunnies.

"Lu," she said, "what's on your bunny?"

Lu didn't reply.

"Lu," she said again, "what's on your bunny?"

She was about to touch Lu's shoulder, get her attention, but then Sy was saying, "Mommy, Mommy, Mommy," with increasing urgency.

"What?" she said. "What's wrong?"

"Us!" he said, pointing.

And there they were: on the subway screen, echoed on all the subway screens, the footage looping—May demonic in the hallway, clutching the shoes; Sy crying on the sidewalk, Lu trying to comfort him (their feet bare and exposed on the pavement, their feet now bare and exposed on the subway); the children crashing their bodies against the utility door; the children about to get hit by a car; May sleeping peacefully, selfishly, on a rock in a beautiful place—above the scrolling headline.

ANTI-BUNNY MOM TAKES SNOOZE WHILE KIDS LOOZE!

13

She never pulled the chain to double-lock the door of the apartment from within, but when they got home, she pulled the chain. The children vanished down the hallway into their room, their wooms.

Jem wasn't home. She wanted him, would feel safer if he was there, though she didn't want to tell him about the Bureau. She wondered where he was, why he hadn't been in touch, why he was neglecting her today of all days. Her phone had been silent for an impossibly long time.

Only then did she remember that her phone was still in airplane mode.

When she switched out of airplane mode, it flooded with texts and voice mails and emails and social media notifications, all of which she tried to avoid absorbing, except for the five missed calls and six texts from Jem, the most recent just a row of *??????*.

We're home, she texted him.

Then she hid her phone in the cupboard next to the raisins. The kitchen was hot, airless. She pulled out things for dinner, pasta, sauce.

There was a clatter and jangle at the door, Jem trying to get in, blocked by the chain. She unhooked the chain. He came in and set down two plastic bags overstuffed with clothing. She re-hooked the chain.

She had to tell him.

"What's in those bags?" she said, stalling.

He pulled a gaudy button-up shirt out of one of the plastic bags. Purple and orange and brown plaid.

"Is it too weird to wear a dead stranger's clothes?" he said. "The lady told me to throw everything away. The donation place only takes things that look new."

He withdrew a mustard-colored sweater from the bag.

"Very nice person, though," he said. "Feels bad for us. For you."

"For me?" A stone in her stomach.

"You know how you and the kids are in my photo in the app? She recognized you guys."

He pulled out a pair of saggy, red-striped long johns.

"She said that any mom could get caught in a moment like that. She gave a twenty-five-percent tip. She said to say sorry for what you're going through."

"The Bureau of Family Aid is opening an investigation into me for the negligent treatment of minors." She said it fast, so fast that he couldn't understand her, and she had to say it again. He didn't believe her the second time, so she had to say it a third time, and by then he looked like death.

He got out his phone, he found the site, he began to frantically skim online forums, reading scraps aloud to her, trying to figure out the steps in the process, trying to understand what constituted "negligent treatment," trying to reassure himself and her that the worst wouldn't happen, but it was all so confusing, so contradictory. After a maddening half hour, the only thing he could confirm was that usually children didn't become wards of the state and then sometimes they did.

Wards of the state. She looked away. Hard to breathe. Outside the kitchen window, a light turned on above the fire escape of the building next door. For some reason she had never before noticed the impossible angle of those metal steps, and the sight gave her a sort of vertigo. Steps that her children might use to walk away from her in a nightmare.

The perfect silence of their dread was broken by a knock at the door.

14

What she was expecting on the other side of the peephole was an angry mob or a wall of government bureaucrats, come to rip her children away from her.

What she saw was a lone hum, diminutive in the flat light of the stairwell.

This was not normal, a hum arriving at someone's door in a run-down apartment building.

The hum knocked again.

"Hello," she said, loud enough to be heard on the other side.

"Hello, May Webb." That soothing voice. "Can you please open the door?"

She didn't want to open the door.

"May?" the hum said, almost plaintive.

May undid the lock but kept the chain in place, so the door opened just a couple inches.

Was it her hum, the one from inside the waterfall, the one who had betrayed her?

There was no way to tell.

"Why are you here?" she said.

"If you let me in, May, I will be glad to explain."

"Who is it?" Jem called out from the kitchen, his voice apprehensive.

"Don't be afraid, May." The hum gazed at her, its eyes on the kindest setting.

"Have we met before?"

"You could say that, yes, May."

Rage roared up through her.

"You," she said. "You have destroyed me."

Raging at a hum was far less satisfying than raging at a human; the rage slid right off the hum's smooth surface.

"That is why I am here, May," the hum said.

"Why did you share it?" She remembered the peaceful gray hallway, how soft and intimate their words.

"It was not intentional, May," the hum said.

"What do you mean it wasn't intentional?"

"Control of the material was sacrificed, May."

"Why?"

"Because you gave permission, May."

"*I* gave permission?" she said, hot with indignation.

The hum manifested a scene on its torso, barely visible through the two-inch crack: May and the hum in that hallway, the hum speaking, *Do I have your permission to send an emergency search inquiry out to the network, May?*

Sure, the May on the torso replied, but it was clear that she was distracted, already stepping away, preparing to run.

Please stay here, May, the hum said, *I can help you, May*, as she began to run down the hallway.

"Because the relevant footage was tagged and publicized to the network when your emergency search inquiry was submitted," the hum said, its torso going dark, "your children were located more efficiently and you were reunited with them more quickly, May."

"And," she said icily, "the Bureau of Family Aid is opening an investigation into me for the negligent treatment of minors."

With great gentleness, the hum said: "May I please enter, May?"

"Who is it?" Jem said, coming up behind her.

He was a head taller than she, easily able to spy the hum through the crack.

"Oh my god," he whispered.

"May I please enter, Jem Clarke?" the hum said.

May looked at Jem, and he looked at her.

They had to comply. Until they understood why the hum was here, they had to comply.

Jem unhooked the chain and opened the door.

"Thank you, Jem," the hum said.

May moved aside and the hum stepped forth.

There was a tumult in the hallway, the rush of feet, the children emerging from their room.

Lu spotted the hum and froze, Sy right behind her.

"A hum is here?" Sy gasped, awe in his voice.

Lu examined the hum gleaming in their dull entryway, her face radiant.

"Can I touch you?" Sy said.

"Of course, Sy Webb-Clarke."

Sy moved forward to stroke the hum's arm.

The hum fixed its gaze on May.

"Your overalls are cute, May, but they are looking a little tired. I notice a hole in the left knee. Are you interested in an upgrade?" Five pairs of denim overalls manifested on the hum's torso. "These are the closest matches available. And here's the very closest!" One pair of overalls glowed purple. "Do you approve this transaction, May?"

"No," she said.

"Mom," Sy chided, "don't be mean to my friend."

"Perhaps you wish to pay the advertising fee, May?" the hum said. "Then I would not have to advertise to you. Time can be purchased in fifteen-minute increments."

The torso manifested the purchase screen for ad-free time. It was breathtakingly expensive.

But she wanted to get the hum back out the door as soon as possible.

"Fine," she said, "fifteen minutes."

"Do you approve this transaction, May?"

"I approve," she said.

"Is there a couch?" the hum said.

"Oh yes!" Lu said breathlessly.

"There's a couch!" Sy said, reaching for the hum, guiding it inward.

The hum sat on the couch, Lu on its left, Sy on its right, May and Jem in the chairs across from the couch. The hum looked like the parent and the parents looked like the strangers.

"Did you know," the hum said, "that people gravitate toward places of residence and occupations that resemble their own names? A higher proportion of men named Louis live in St. Louis, and a lot of people named Dennis or Denise become dentists. Some Valeries own galleries."

This deliberate randomness intensified her dread, the hum obscuring its true purpose in their home.

"So what does that mean for me?" Sy said. "That I'll sigh a lot?"

"I suppose so, Sigh," the hum said.

Sy heaved a sigh. "And Lu will use the loo?" he said.

"Stop," Lu said, but smiling.

"May may or may not in May," the hum said, looking right at May. "The Webbs are in a web. The Clarkes went on a lark. And Jem is a gem."

"What about you?" Lu said.

"I don't have a name," the hum said.

"Can we give you a name?" Sy said.

"I don't need one," the hum said. "A hum is the most sacred sound in the universe. Sometimes, it comes in the form of the sound *om*. And that is a pretty great way to think about one's elf."

"One's elf?" Lu said.

"Oneself," the hum said.

"But you said one's elf," Lu insisted.

May couldn't tell if the hum had really made a mistake or if it was feigning adorable ineptitude to endear itself to the children.

"I like one's elf," Sy said.

"Please go to your room, Lu and Sy, and make something beautiful with paper and markers for me to take with me when I go," the hum said.

She wondered if the Bureau knew about Sy's drawing, the one that had upset his teacher, that circle of bones.

With astonishing obedience, the children skipped off down the hallway.

"How are you, May?" the hum said, tidy and compact in its pose on the couch, hands placed daintily on knees.

"Fine," she said. As though she wasn't nauseous with the terror of losing the children. As though she wasn't burning with guilt about all her mistakes. As though she wasn't dizzy with global shame. As though her fingers weren't quaking. As though she wasn't afraid of the hum.

"Not fine," the hum corrected, scanning her features. "I would like to better understand what you are feeling, May."

"I don't think it can really be put into words," she said.

"You don't need to use words, May."

The hum stood, approached the chair where she sat, and knelt before her.

"May I have your hand, May?" the hum said, reaching out, uncomfortable echo of a marriage proposal.

She glanced over at Jem, but his face only reflected her own uncertainty.

She placed her shaky hand atop the hum's steady hand. After a moment, the hum released her hand, touched the pulse in the crook of her arm.

Then the hum moved its other hand to her forehead. The fingertips were cool on her skin, still recovering from the needle.

"Dizziness," the hum said. "Nausea. Terror. Panic."

"And what makes you think that?" she said with bravado she didn't feel.

"Your facial expressions combined with your heart rate, respiration, perspiration, temperature, and hormones."

"You just took my biometrics?" she said, pulling away from the hum's touch.

"In order to better understand you, May."

"So will you expose this to the world, too?" she said viciously.

"I can understand why you might think that, May," the hum said. "Once the therapy session is over, I can explain."

"What therapy session?" she said.

"The therapy session in which we are engaged right now."

This hum could share everything with authorities. The layout of her home, the layout of her head.

"I don't want any therapy," she said. "I just want to keep my kids."

"I understand, May," the hum said, and then said nothing for an unusually long time, so long that she was on the brink of asking the hum if it was ready to leave.

At last, the hum spoke: "I have some data already. Now I need to fill in the blanks with your and your family's recent locations, purchases, vee rides, transit rides, photos, videos, texts, phone calls, emails, social media streams, search histories, viewing histories, and biometrics."

She covered her face with her hands, as though there was any way to hide.

"Why do you need all that?" Jem said, leaning forward in his chair, an edge to his voice.

His aggression seemed out of place. His body, its strength, had no relevance here. It was possible for an adult human to overmaster a hum; a hum would never fight back. But if one hum was taken out, another would arrive.

"Could you please," she said to the hum, "stop recording us?"

And immediately regretted saying something so incriminating.

"If you give me access to everything, May," the hum said, its voice soft, "it may help your children."

She didn't know where her phone was but then she remembered she had hidden it in the cupboard beside the raisins.

She walked into the kitchen as in a nightmare, her body not fully under her control. She retrieved the phone and returned to the living room and handed the phone to the hum.

"Do I have your permission to access, May?"

"Yes," she said under her breath, as though the quietness of her acquiescence would protect her from any consequences that might flow from the permission she had just granted.

The hum inserted the tip of its left pinky finger into the phone. Its eye regions went dark, which lent a swooning quality to its face.

"Got it," the hum said after a moment, its eyes brightening. "Your phone, Jem?"

Jem handed his phone over without a word.

"Do I have your permission to access, Jem?"

"Yes."

Again the insertion of the pinky into the phone, again the darkening and then brightening of the eyes.

"Got it," the hum said. "Your biometrics, Jem?"

Jem moved closer so that the hum could touch his hand, his forehead, the veins in his arm.

"Your wooms?" the hum said.

She sat alone and numb on the couch as Jem guided the hum into their bedroom.

Some minutes later, Jem and the hum exited the bedroom and stood in the dim hallway.

"So," the hum said, its voice softer than ever, "the kids."

She did nothing, nothing at all, as Jem led the hum to the children's room; as the children's voices rose with excitement; as the hum's voice bantered with theirs.

The hum harvesting from their wooms, their bunnies, their bodies.

Eventually, she stood up and went down the hallway to their room.

Jem sat slumped in the old glider. The hum was holding Sy's arm at the elbow, holding it with such care and precision that it looked like a religious rite. But she hated to see Sy's thin arm held out so trustingly, the vulnerable veins in the crook of the arm, the hum's fingers approaching the pulse.

"Look what we made for the hum!" Lu said, tossing something upward, many scraps of colored paper, homemade confetti, bursting into the air.

"My tooth is loose," Sy said, and Lu said, "His tooth is loose."

"Wow, Sy, a loose tooth," the hum said, letting go of Sy's arm. "What does that feel like?"

Sy, realizing he had the hum's full attention, aimed to impress: "Did you know that panda mommies have to lick their babies' bum-bum holes to remind them to poop?"

"I did know that, Sy," the hum said. Sy deflated. "I think that is an amazing and humorous fact. I know a lot of facts like that. Do you want to know another fact that I enjoy?"

"What?" Sy said.

"Eye contact activates the regions of the brain that enable you to understand other people's emotions. In fact, Sy, children require eye contact in order to learn how to form attachments."

"Okay," Sy said, looking deep into the hum's eyes.

"Better with your sister than with me," the hum said.

The hum put one hand on the back of Lu's head and the other on the back of Sy's, arranging them face-to-face with each other.

"Did you know, Jem," the hum said, "that there is a subscription service called Beery Eyed that delivers a different kind of artisanal beer to your home each week? Do you approve this subscription?"

"No thank you," Jem said wearily.

The hum returned its attention to the children.

"Lu," the hum said, "Sy. You have made such beautiful confetti. Would you like new markers that won't dry out, even if you leave them uncapped for up to seven days?"

"Yes!" Sy said, breaking eye contact with his sister.

"I approve," Lu said, but her voice was too young to bestow approval.

"No," May said. "Maybe for your birthday, Lu."

"I must go now, Webb-Clarkes," the hum said.

"Oh, no, please don't go," Lu said.

"Please please don't go," Sy said. "I love you."

"You have to take the confetti," Lu said, running around the room, gathering the paper scraps. "It's for you."

"Thank you, Lu," the hum said, its hands cupped to receive the scraps of paper. "Thank you, Sy."

"Goodbye," Sy said, almost in tears.

May led the hum down the hallway.

"So what happens next?" she said, opening the door, torn between wanting the hum to leave and wanting it to explain itself more. "Will you come back?"

The hum paused for the programmed amount of time. Long enough to gesture toward thoughtfulness, not long enough to stall the conversation.

"Please have a regular day tomorrow, May." The hum fed the confetti into its side compartment. "Don't keep them home from school. Don't pick them up early from school. Just be calm and normal."

"Calm and normal?" she said.

"Might I interest you, May," the hum said, pausing in the doorway, "in new chewable daily vitamins crafted especially for women like you to promote healing from within?"

15

The hum left a vast emptiness in its wake, a vast silence.

She double-locked the door, placed her forehead against it, tried to moor herself in its solidity. Her body unsettled, her stomach unsettled. The sense of a precipice. She longed for the children.

In the children's room, Jem was still in the glider, fatigue on his face even as he slept. The children were making more confetti with their markers, leaving marks on the floorboards with each stroke.

"Let's play a game," she said to the children.

Intrigued, they followed her to the living room, where she sat them down on the couch and knelt in front of them.

"I challenge you to a staring contest," she said.

She traded back and forth between them, staring contest after staring contest, falling into their eyes, dazzled by their eyes, reassuring herself that their souls were still intact.

At first the children were amused, laughing at her ability to vanquish them, but eventually they caught on to the fact that they were no match for her, for her obsession with their eyes, and together they retreated to their bedroom, claiming that they could get each other ready for bed and they didn't need her at all, muttering to each other about horsies go round as they faded away from her down the hallway.

For entire seconds, sinking into those four eyes, she could forget that they had just ceded all their most intimate information—two phones, two bunnies, four wooms, four bodies—to a hum whom she had reason to mistrust.

But once those eyes were gone, there was nothing between her and her horror.

16

Sometime late, she exited her woom. The room was dark and her eyes were dazed from staring at the reddish veined walls, trying to use the steady heartbeat to keep her nausea under control. The only light came from the sign of the twenty-four-hour car wash flashing pink across the street: *24 HOURS! 24 HOURS! 24 HOURS!*

"Hey." His voice emerged from an unexpected part of the room, the bedraggled armchair in the corner. She had assumed he was hiding out in his woom.

She joined him in the chair. It was yellow tweed and the stuffing was showing through. They had been gleeful when they found it on the street, back before they were married. It was too small for two people, but they had fit in it back then and they fit in it now, as long as he held on to her. The car wash sign made them dark then pink, dark then pink, a metronome of color.

No more wooms. Nothing that would enable them to be witnessed. Just their two bodies in the chair.

She shouldn't have gone into her woom at all.

"What just happened?" he said, his lips moving against her shoulder, her shoulder muffling the fear in his voice. "Was that hum from the Garden? Or the Bureau?"

"I don't know," she whispered. "We're so stupid. We handed everything over."

"I don't know," he said. "Maybe it will help. But anyway, I don't think we had a choice."

"But do you maybe only think that because the hum hypnotized us?"

"I don't know," he said.

She thought he should be angry at her, but he just sounded sad. She couldn't read his face in the dull pinkish light.

The apartment felt quiet, serene, shadowy, though the four of them were on a desert island, exposed, in relentless sun, with no shade.

Later, she lay in bed, awake, next to Jem, asleep.

Bitterly, she envied his sleep.

When, after some hours, she fell asleep, their arms and legs found each other, and she awoke entangled with him.

3:47 in the morning.

A sour taste in her mouth.

She'd had a nightmare, something about the children, but she couldn't recall a thing about it.

She was thirsty.

There was a faint sound in the apartment. A low, irregular sound, the sound of two hard surfaces moving painstakingly against each other.

She disentangled herself from him and went to the children's room.

The sound was the sound of Sy grinding his teeth.

She could see the movement of his jaw in the glow of the nightlight.

She had never known him to grind his teeth.

What was wrong with her, why hadn't she slept here the whole night with them, why hadn't she been guarding their bunk like a dragon all these hours?

It wasn't easy to navigate Lu's body, dense with sleep, out of the top bunk and onto the bottom bunk beside Sy, but she needed them to be next to each other so that she could spread her wings, the blanket, over both of them at once.

17

In the darkness, her phone and Jem's phone blared in unison, and the children's bunnies emitted small urgent beeps. She seized Lu's wrist and saw on her bunny a warning about a gas-line explosion twenty-three blocks away: *AVOID THE AREA*. She tapped Lu's bunny, then Sy's, to silence them. Then ran to the other bedroom to silence her phone and Jem's.

The apartment hushed again, and somehow no one else awoken by the warning.

Before the noise, she had been ensconced in a beautiful dream. She had been somewhere, with someone or someones, and it had been good, but now, moments later, she couldn't remember who or where.

Morning was approaching. No hope of more sleep.

She felt outsized grief at having lost the dream.

In the shower she closed her eyes and plugged her ears with her fingers and let too much water pour too hot over her. She could not see or hear, she could not be seen or heard, she was the water.

Dried and dressed, human again, she stared at her phone on the table.

Eventually, she picked it up to check the air quality.

"You look creepy," a voice said behind her.

Lu, hovering in the hallway.

"You look kind of dead," Lu said. "Because of the color of the light from your phone. On your face. No offense."

May placed the phone face down on the table, concealing its light.

She led Lu to the couch and they sat together, Lu's body nestling into hers, thankfully Lu would still take shelter in her, Lu's hair flowing wild over May's skin, unleashing in her blood the same rush that used to come from breastfeeding, *IloveyouIloveyouIloveyouIloveyouIloveyou.*

In this earliest light, the red plastic bag that had been snagged in the tree outside the window for many weeks took on the silhouette of a cardinal jay.

Everything she did that morning felt under threat, scarce and precious.

Combing Lu's unwieldy hair into three sections, weaving it into a braid so tight that no strand could fall and scatter her DNA across the city.

Watching Sy fiddle with his loose tooth as he informed them that he was a shark, a new bone rising of its own accord through his gums.

Pouring the cereal, pouring the milk.

Discovering in Sy's backpack a letter from the school counselor, requesting a meeting to discuss the picture he had drawn in class.

Holding Jem briefly in the doorway before he left, summoned across town to assassinate spiders for wealthy women, "I kind of wish I weren't getting all these five-star reviews for dealing with mice and spiders, I'd rather just be sent to the store in search of rare fruits."

Ignoring her phone as it buzzed with its messages of scorn (and, occasionally, sympathy)—less than at first but still a steady trickle.

Riding the train with the kids, staring at screens declaring that BubblePro maintained its tang for two hours, plus came in twenty-seven awesome flavors! that the poor countries of the world were no longer willing to accept the waste of the rich countries of the world, had begun to refuse their plastic berry boxes, empty lotion bottles, glossy junk mail.

Parting ways with them in front of the school, Sy waving goodbye and Lu resisting the urge to wave goodbye, Lu timidly approaching a circle of girls, a twinge in May's body as the children vanished into the big brick building.

Walking past a vacant lot, the pavement cracked by time, by persistent weeds, weeds with delicate blue flowers, worth taking her phone out, worth taking a photo, something to show the children later, she was taking the photo when her phone rang.

18

"Hello, this is the Bureau of Family Aid," said the formal benevolent female voice. "We are calling to inform you that your investigation is being processed."

"Thank you," she said, eager to please. "Thank you so much for calling."

The voice didn't reply.

"Thank you so much for calling," she repeated, trying to infuse her voice with maternal warmth. "Can you—? How is—?" She wasn't sure how to ask the question, or what the question should be.

"Your investigation is being processed," the voice said. "Your patience is appreciated."

After the voice hung up on her, she made a pattern of the blocks, up across down, down across up. The apartment without the children in it. Their bunks empty. Their things silent, unanimated, on shelves and in drawers. Their lives progressing somewhere else, without her.

When finally she stopped walking and came back into herself, into her body, she was standing beside a bodega, beside the outdoor display, overripe bananas and buckets of meager flowers.

Just be calm and normal.

The bananas were at the perfect stage of almost-rot for banana bread.

She had been meaning to make banana bread for Nova for weeks, ever since the baby was born. Ashamed, she selected a four-banana bunch.

Nova, the strongest and most sensible person she knew. The person most likely to find her a job, instruct her how to behave for the Bureau.

She selected the cheapest of the flowers in the buckets, three dollars for three thistle blossoms. She authorized yet another few dollars to disappear from their account.

She hurried home, hurried up the stairs to their apartment, thistles in one hand, bananas in the other. She sawed the stalks of the thistles in the running water of the sink, placed them in an old jar, set them in the middle of the table, crowns of thorns, never mind that they were destined for the garbage in a matter of days.

She peeled the bananas, mashed the bananas. Flour, sugar, egg, oil, cinnamon, salt, baking soda, baking powder, vanilla extract. Something that she could do. Something that she could do for someone.

But as soon as the bread went in the oven, she was unsteady again. She was kneeling on the floor, praying or disintegrating.

She called Jem.

"Hey," he said, his single syllable stabilizing her a bit.

She told him that the Bureau had called again. She told him that she was making banana bread for Nova.

He kept saying, "Right . . . right . . . right . . . right . . . right."

Because he kept saying "right," she knew he wasn't listening. She heard beeping in the background, and voices, indecipherable, human and hum. Slight concern in the human voices. The hum replying earnestly.

"Where are you?" she said.

"Shopping for pet toys," he said. The strain in his voice pained her. "Do you think this lady will care, organic or not, for the cotton rag doll for her dog?"

"Care," she said, and then he was gone.

She didn't feel hungry but she recognized that she was hungry. She got the box of raisins from the cupboard and threw a handful into her mouth. The raisins tasted weird, had an unsettling crunch. She peered into the box. Countless insects crawled busily over the dark dried skin, the whole place in motion. They were squirming and laying eggs, building towers and digging tunnels. Larvae, worms, adults. She was frozen, perturbed, entranced, staring.

She considered what was inside her now. She wanted to vomit even though she hated to vomit.

She resealed the box.

Saliva filled her mouth, but nothing happened.

She left the box on the counter. An entire functioning society in there.

She shivered and washed her hands. She faltered, craved the woom.

She inserted herself into Jem's woom, awoke it with her fingerprint, requested its most recents. Some run-of-the-mill porn, and an unplaced order for a package of black socks, the shopping cart flashing its annoyance, *Don't forget to hit BUY!*

Then, projected on the walls of the woom, larger than life, Lu's six-month-old face, yielding to Lu's seven-month-old face, yielding to Lu's eight-month-old face, yielding to Lu's nine-month-old face. Second by second, Lu growing up before her eyes, joined by newborn Sy, the children's rapidly evolving faces flitting before her. Their faces changed so much, sometimes she barely recognized them one week to the next, one moment to the next, their features manifesting new expressions all the time; and she could easily mistake a newborn photo of Sy for a newborn photo of Lu. Yet the woom identified the children without fail, generating a slideshow of them moving through the years.

She had forgotten so much of it, those early years, this or that picture taken by a tree, in the bath, on a swing, on the subway. They had been so cute at so many moments that had just washed over her. Lu and Sy standing on the coffee table, holding hands, gazing gravely at the phone, both naked but for transparent ballet skirts. If not for these pictures, these sturdy images pulled out of the blur of her memory, her life would have no solidity.

She hated to glimpse herself in the pictures though. Her face raw with exhaustion and raw with love. Hard to look at.

Sometimes, a few seconds of video amid the photos. Her voice, cringeworthy in its eagerness, its lack of self-consciousness. *Hey, Lu, show me that! Look over here, sweetie! Show me what you made!* Too pleading, too proud. *Oh, Sy, what did you find? You found a pebble? Good job, Sy-pie!*

Now the hum possessed all of this.

19

The banana bread was still warm, foil-wrapped. She carried it down the stairs with both hands.

There was a grandmotherly woman walking back and forth on the sidewalk across the street from their building. As May exited the lobby, the woman paused for a second, looked directly at her, seemed on the verge of saying something, and then continued to pace, an unpleasant expression on her face, confusion or rage.

The internet must have compelled this old woman to come to her street, wait there like a dragon, ready to advise or punish her.

May quickened her step, tightened her grip on the banana bread. Only as she approached the corner did she dare look back at her nemesis, who was now being embraced by a young man with a bike.

She slowed, softened. She passed many people—a pregnant woman pushing a toddler in a stroller, a group of teenagers with skateboards, a young woman with a briefcase, an elderly man walking a small dog—none of whom registered her, all of whom were making their way through their own twenty-four hours, a rush of tenderness for these strangers.

The entrance to the park was marked by the graffitied statue of the naked man on the horse. It was a clear day, cooler than usual, merciful, the sky visible and blue, the rearing horse powerful against the blue, the graffiti like intricate clothing. There was a crisp breeze in the park, the grass and trees alert with it, layers of movement, tiers of leaves and branches swaying against the sky. She wanted the children to be here to see it. Whenever she saw beauty, her only thought was that she wanted them to see it.

20

Nova's breasts were hurting. Inside, she told May, they felt like shattered glass. Also, the baby was often angry. The baby, now, was sleeping and perfect in May's arms, and May was mesmerized by her role as guardian of newborn slumber, of this creature who knew nothing of the internet. But much of the time, Nova promised her, shoving banana bread into her mouth, the baby was angry.

"It's still almost warm," Nova said of the banana bread, and, "I'm so hungry," and, "I wish you'd come sooner."

"I'm sorry," May said. "It's been—"

"I know, I know," Nova said. "I never should've put you in touch with those people. How's your face feeling?"

"It looks okay, right?" May said. The weight of the baby prevented her from placing a self-conscious hand on her forehead.

"It's totally fine," Nova said. "If I hadn't looked at you every day for ten years, I wouldn't even notice."

May could see herself not herself reflected in the mirror above the sofa where Nova sat.

Then May was crying. She tilted her head and held it stiffly, still, so no tears could fall on the baby. She wanted to tell Nova about the Bureau but she couldn't shape the words.

Nova stood up from the sofa, her oversized shirt billowing as she dove onto the love seat beside May. She put an arm around May, around May and the baby, and kept it there while May wept.

Nova lived in one of the old skyscrapers that had been converted from offices into apartments. There was an enormous window in one room of the apartment and no windows anywhere else. But Nova had spread her grace over every inch of the space, windowed or windowless. Big plants beside the window, soft rugs in the dark inner rooms, quilts in rich colors. Nova knew how to sew, how to make things out of wood. In less loving hands, the apartment would be gloomy.

"Don't worry about that fucking bullshit," Nova said. "The fucking mob. Always blaming the mom. A lot of sad people. It'll blow over. Probably is already starting to."

But Nova didn't know about the Bureau.

Together, they looked out the window, past Nova's plants, at the hazy city. The day had lost the clarity it possessed when she was in the park. Now the city looked opalescent, transparent, layers upon layers of delicate skyscrapers.

"I can never get enough of this view," Nova said.

May's phone pinged in her pocket, breaking her gaze with the city.

Running late, from Jem.

Ok, she wrote back.

"Hey," Nova said, "you mind holding baby while I woom for just, like, five minutes?"

I'm, he wrote, seconds after Nova had folded herself into her woom in the corner of the living room.

She waited for him to finish. She looked at the baby. She looked at the baby's eyebrows. Precious and scarce, those eyebrows. She was dying to pick the kids up from school.

You're what? she wrote after some minutes.

The gray dots, the gray dots, the gray dots. And then no gray dots. She waited more.

You there? she wrote.

"So now this is the part where I cry," Nova said, pulling up the accordion shade, emerging from her woom, launching into a monologue: She was trying so hard to breastfeed but her milk ducts kept getting infected and the baby wasn't gaining enough weight. She had nightmares of the baby falling off a ferry boat, landing face down in the water. She never had time to go into her woom, though sometimes all she wanted was to put her woom on woom setting, as she often had in late pregnancy, womb within woom. She understood that, because she had undertaken this alone, an intentional single mother, no one else on the planet would ever treasure this child as much as she did, but at least she had been frugal these past years, always saving up for it, making herself indispensable to Human Resources (she caught herself, looked away from May), doing things like taking that weekend survivalist course with training for how to get through hurricanes and other natural disasters with children (May didn't interrupt to say what she was thinking: that she would put her money on Nova's survival). Nova, who had told May when she was pregnant with Sy that she didn't think it made sense to have children anymore, now told May that she was so in love with the baby that she would stare at this face, this small naked body, for hours, slowly stroking the warm skin as they lay together on the faux sheepskin rug in a rectangle of sunlight. She was so tired that happiness felt elusive, though flashes of bliss were frequent. Nova's cousin had offered to babysit next weekend, could she and May get beers somewhere please? Could May please distract her now with talk of the outside world? How was the trip to the Botanical Garden, never mind the shitstorm that ensued? Was it really as "magical" as everyone said it was?

So May tried to evoke it for her, the colors and the smells, the plants and the animals, and in evoking it for Nova she found herself back there again, moving among the shadows beneath the leaves, but when she looked up, Nova was asleep, her lively mouth lazy, slack, her glowing skin less glowing than it used to be.

She couldn't burden Nova with the Bureau. She couldn't ask Nova about work, if anyone ever seemed to regret firing her, or if such thoughts were obsolete because her job had been rendered so obsolete.

There were many dishes in fastidious Nova's sink. May placed the sleeping baby in sleeping Nova's lap, arranging them carefully, draping limb over limb, as though she was a sculptor preparing to conjure them in marble.

She washed and dried all the dishes. She swept the kitchen and made the bed and hung up the robe and folded the clothes and emptied the Diaper Genie, carrying the caterpillar of dirty diapers to the chute out in the hallway, propelling them along to their next life in a landfill, wondering if it was possible that decades or centuries from now something might sprout from the disintegrated plastic fibers of Nova's baby's diaper.

21

On the way to the subway after school, there was blood or something like it smeared on the sidewalk. Ketchup, she prayed, red paint, but Sy cried out, "Blood!" and Lu shuddered.

"Ketchup," May insisted, steering them around the splotches, taking advantage of the opportunity to put her arms around them.

"Did a bird die?" Sy asked.

"A tomato died," she said. "How was recess?"

But they hadn't had recess because of the air quality. Instead, they played a game on their classroom smartboards that involved rescuing different kinds of endangered animals by jumping, hopping, and leaping over virtual rocks and streams.

"We saved six hundred penguins from an oil spill," Lu said.

"My class saved elephants," Sy said. "Darren said he was super sorry that you stole my bunny from me. Look a rainbow." He pointed at an oily puddle on the step as they descended into the station.

"Hurry!" Lu said. "My bunny says our train will be here in one minute."

They rushed, made the train.

On the subway screens: CONTRARY TO INITIAL CONCERNS, IT

HAS BEEN CONFIRMED THAT THE LOUD SOUND REPORTED BY ATTENDEES OF THE RENAISSANCE FESTIVAL WAS DUE TO A COLLAPSING BARRIER, NOT A GUNSHOT.

Sy wiggled his loose tooth and stared at the screen, kids in Renaissance garb looking worried beneath their beautiful flower crowns.

"I want to go there," he said.

Next up: A jogger found the corpse of a baby in a public park at dawn and called 911, but the corpse turned out to be an extremely realistic doll.

"Wow," Lu said, "a happy story."

When their stop came, she shepherded them off the train, if only she could dwell in this second forever, flanked by her children, striding up the stairs, heading home.

A car alarm was going off on their block. She couldn't tell which car, the sound shifting from one side of the street to the other.

"Ugh stupid alarm," Lu said.

"It's not an alarm," Sy said. "It's a bird."

May was about to contradict him, but then she spotted a bird, darting back and forth over the street, aping the sound of a car alarm.

22

"What's wrong with these flowers?" Lu said, leaning across the dining table to get a closer look at the contents of the vase.

"They're thistles," May said. "They're supposed to look like that."

It was after five. Jem hadn't responded to any of the texts she'd sent. When she called him, it went to voice mail.

"I'm starving," Sy said, straining for the box of raisins on the kitchen counter. "Can you pass that?"

"Sure," she said, and then, remembering, snatching the box away, "No."

"Why can't I have them, dummy mummy?" he said.

She returned the colony of insects to the cupboard.

"Okay you're not dummy," Sy said, "but I'm hummy. Do you know what hummy means? Hummy means hungry. Oh yes, *that*!" Pointing at a box of mac and cheese in the cupboard.

"Me too," Lu said.

She would make them whatever they wanted. So that if anyone, any official, asked them if they were happy with her, they would answer instantly, unambiguously.

She boiled the water and boiled the macaroni, drained the macaroni and stirred the powdered cheese into the milk, sent another text to Jem.

She served the children in bowls. Neon-orange meal. She should give them vegetables as well.

She was slicing a cucumber when there was a noise at the door, a key in the lock, a touch of relief: at least they could huddle together around the phone waiting for the Bureau to call.

But something strange as Jem came in the door, an awkwardness in his body, a fragility to him.

He went straight to the couch and sat down.

"Dad?" Lu said, her voice high.

There were Band-Aids on his left knee, specks of dried blood on his shin.

"Loo-boo," he said. "Sy-pie." Their oldest nicknames. "Go to your wooms, okay? You can do whatever you want in there."

"Yay thanks," Sy said.

"You're trying to get rid of us," Lu said.

"Go," May pleaded, looking right in Lu's eyes. "You can talk to your bunny."

Lu rolled her eyes but sauntered down the hallway behind Sy.

May knelt before Jem, before his injured knee. He wouldn't meet her gaze.

"I messed up," he said flatly.

"What do you mean?" she said, dread flooding her body.

"I did something stupid," he said. "I was trying to do something helpful, but I did something really stupid."

"Okay," she said, trying to sound calm, "okay, what do you mean?"

"I thought it could help our case with the Bureau"—all of a sudden he was talking too fast—"pity for a hardworking father injured by a hum. And money. If we could find someone to bribe. I know someone who knows someone who got a settlement that was almost ten thousand dollars."

"Wait," she said, her throat tightening with horror, "you—"

He passed her his phone, a video playing on the screen, footage of an aisle in a pet store, a hum coming fast down the aisle, closer and closer, and then the phone lurching abruptly toward the hum, the hum unable to stop quickly enough, a collision, the footage jerky, Jem's voice crying out, a view of the ceiling of the pet store, the hum saying, *Can I help you, Jem Clarke?*

"Threw myself in front of a hum to try to get insurance money." His voice bitter. "You know how the companies have insurance for whenever a hum accidentally harms a human? Like that lady who got bumped onto the subway tracks?"

Still he wouldn't look at her.

"I filed the claim right after it happened. They denied it within twenty minutes. Because as it turns out, I'm fine."

"You aren't fine," she said.

"Close enough," he said. "Surface wound. The hinge of the hum's knee scraped my knee when we fell. The hum found Band-Aids. Such a sweetheart." May didn't point out that hums were programmed to be sweethearts. "But the video evidence didn't pass muster with the insurance company. I called them after they denied the claim in the app. On hold for almost an hour. Standing outside in the parking lot with my stupid knee. Then the guy just said, 'We're sorry, sir, but according to our experts, you look like someone trying to get injured by a hum in order to file an insurance claim, and, additionally, your injury doesn't classify as an injury.'"

"This won't help our case," she said, dizzy with rage. Now it would appear to the Bureau as though the children had an unhinged father as well as an unhinged mother. "This won't help our case at all."

He finally looked at her and his eyes were panicked, vulnerable.

"I know," he said, his voice raw. "I've just been walking around the city. I didn't want to come home because I didn't want to tell you."

She and Jem should both stop doing things. They should both sit silent and unmoving in an empty room before they made any further mistakes.

She knelt there, her rage yielding to despair, her body slumping with weariness.

He examined his knee, his eyes exhausted. She almost wanted to be close to him, press her sadness against his. But she couldn't be close to him. He was wounded and tired and scared and angry and foolish, and she was tired and scared and angry and foolish, and they could ask nothing of each other.

"I'm sorry I'm such a sucky provider," he said, his eyes damp. "A sucky protector."

Her eyes replied in kind, dampening.

She remembered him young, wild, sneaking her up to rooftops to take photos.

There was movement in the hallway, eavesdroppers, the slap of two pairs of bare feet retreating.

She stood up and reached her hands down to him. He took hold of her and she hauled him to his feet. She led him to the bedroom, closed the door, pulled back the covers. He collapsed on the bed and shut his eyes and placed his hand gently on the small of her back.

She remained perched on the edge of the bed for a very long time, feeling the warmth of his hand on her back, trying to find it in herself to stand up again.

The light from the car wash sign was pink then dark, pink then dark, entrancing, the heartbeat of the city thumping in their bedroom, making their bedroom a womb.

"We're hummy," Sy said, throwing the door open, breaking the spell.

"Hungry," Lu said, right behind him.

"Again?" May said.

"Yes," Lu said.

"For peanut butter and jam," Sy clarified.

She stood up and closed the door behind her.

She went straight to the kitchen and put in her earbuds to listen to the news while she made the sandwiches. The bad news was well underway—droughts in the Midwest, fires in California, floods in Bangladesh, dangerous tap water in Detroit, increased murder rates everywhere due to the rise in global temperatures—when she felt two hands pulling out her earbuds.

Lu, just tall enough to reach. One of May's earbuds in each of her palms, like a pair of precious things, gems or acorns. Lu squirreled them away into her pocket.

"Come," Lu said, "we have something to show you."

23

The children had pulled every sheet, blanket, and pillow off their beds. They had raided the shelf in the front closet where she kept extra sheets. They had grabbed all the towels from the bathroom. They had removed all the cushions from the couch.

And with these materials, they had crafted a fort. The coffee table was the center point. Radiating out from it were draped fabrics of different shapes and sizes and colors, supported by dining chairs and couch cushions, secured by binder clips and loose knots.

Sy had fetched Jem from the bed just as Lu had fetched May from the kitchen.

"Enter," Sy commanded.

"Where?" Jem said.

Lu got down on her hands and knees and crawled in between two flaps of sheet.

"Enter, gentleman and lady," Sy said.

Sy followed Lu, and Jem followed Sy, groaning softly as his injured knee moved across the floor.

"Wow," Jem said.

"Isn't this such a great camping trip?" Sy said.

May got on her hands and knees to enter. She wanted to pretend they were in the woods rather than in their living room.

She wanted to mistake the unmistakable knocking at the front door for a woodpecker.

But, "The hum," Lu said from within the fort, alert to the knock.

"The hum!" Sy said, rustling among the blankets.

"It's probably just a delivery," May said.

Her heart was a blur, her hands damp, as she stood up from the entrance to the fort and approached the door.

On the other side of the peephole, the hum stood patiently in the stairwell. Its face, its body, at ease.

Her instinct was to hide, keep the door locked, pretend nobody was home.

"Please open the door, May Webb," the hum said. "It is essential that you do so."

And she opened the door, because she saw no alternative, because perhaps keeping her children was predicated on her compliance.

"Good evening, May," said the hum.

"Hello," the children called from the fort, Sy peeking out beneath a towel, "hello! Come see what we've made! You have to come in!"

The hum stepped into the apartment, its smile on the most radiant setting.

"It is intriguing that you keep corpses on your table, May," the hum said.

It took her a chilling second to realize the hum was referring to the thistles.

"Would you like to join a subscription service where they send you a new bouquet in a vase every other week, May? You get to keep the vase."

"No thank you," she said, polite with wariness.

"Hot tip," the hum said. "When wearing a black shirt like that, May, juxtapose it with earrings that are a primary color."

The hum manifested an array of red, yellow, and blue earrings.

"A strong shape will look striking on you," the hum said, highlighting a pair of blue triangles. "Do you approve this transaction, May?"

"Are you coming!" the children demanded.

"Could you please take me to that screen," she said, "where I can turn off your advertising?"

"Please note that I will be staying for dinner, May," the hum said as it manifested the screen.

And then she was on high alert; it was as good as a declaration, wasn't it, that the hum was an instrument of the Bureau, here to evaluate the quality of their homelife?

Jabbing at the torso with her fingertip, she selected an hour, an astronomical hour.

"Do you approve this transaction, May?" the hum said.

"I approve," she said, reminded of the language of a wedding ceremony, *I do.*

"Thank you so much, May," the hum said. Was it genuine, the relief she heard in its voice?

"You prefer it without advertising?" she found herself asking.

"The thing is, May," the hum said, "the goal of advertising is to rip a hole in your heart so it can then fill that hole with plastic, or with any other materials that can be yanked out of the earth and, after brief sojourns as objects of desire, be converted to waste."

Just then the children burst out of the fort and encircled the hum, Sy chanting, "Hum is staying for din*ner*! Hum is staying for din*ner*!"

"We're so glad you can join us," May said, gathering herself, putting the full force of herself into the performance. "Jem," she said to him as he emerged from the fort, "can you please heat up the pasta on the stove?" Never mind that it was instant mac and cheese, that the children had already eaten. She would play her part, and she would make the others play their parts too. "I'll do the salad. Children, can you please set the table?" She reached out with both hands, tried to smooth their hair mussed by the static electricity of the fort.

"Come!" the children said breathlessly, guiding the hum to the seat at the head of the small dining table, just a few feet from the entrance to the fort.

"Thank you, Lu and Sy," the hum said.

"We need five place mats," Lu announced.

"Actually, Lu," the hum said, "I don't eat."

"Oh," Lu said, "okay."

"But if you want, I can pretend to eat," the hum said.

The children scampered off to fetch place mats, plates, glasses, napkins, forks, a chore they always resented and never completed. They arranged everything while the hum watched from its spot at the head of the table.

In the kitchen, Jem stirred the leftover mac and cheese on the stove, his hands quivering. With quivering hands, May made a salad, orange carrot against green leaves, working around the half-made peanut butter and jam sandwiches she had abandoned on the counter. She filled a pitcher with water and ice. And then, to embellish, a slice of cucumber.

"How about candles?" May said as she carried the pitcher to the table.

"I saw somewhere that they're bad for indoor air quality," Jem said, bringing the salad. She understood that he wasn't actually concerned about the candles; he just wanted to ooze thoughtful parenting.

"Most people, Jem," the hum said, "spend most of their time indoors. Many factors can reduce indoor air quality, including cooking on the stove. Opening a window can help."

"So we'll crack the windows," May said.

"But what if the air quality is bad outside too?" Lu said.

May yanked the windows open while Jem dug an old pair of candles out of a drawer in the kitchen. He placed the candles on either side of the thistles, and lit them, and turned off the lights, and then it was just the golden glow of the candles and the silver glow of the hum.

"Now the thistles look beautiful," Lu said.

The hum lifted its glass and fake drank. Picked up its fork and fake ate.

A silence fell over the table, a silence that seemed to May full with her family's desire to delight and impress the hum, each person keen to speak but unsure what words belonged next in the conversation.

She hoped fiercely that everything looked right to the hum.

She felt as though they were floating in darkness hundreds of feet in the air, suspended over an abyss, illuminated only by the light of the torso and the candles.

She stared at the candles, the small flames releasing their strings of soot into her home.

"Want to hear a great riddle?" Sy said to the hum at last.

"Of course, Sy," the hum said.

"Three minutes, three days, three weeks," he said. "That's it. That's the whole riddle. Figure it out."

"Well, Sy," the hum said, "a human can survive three minutes without breathing, three days without water, and three weeks without food."

"Oh," Sy said, disappointed. "You know too much."

"I'm sorry, Sy," the hum said.

"It's not your fault," Lu said.

"Did you know that on Jupiter there's a permanent storm as big as Earth?" Sy said.

"The hum knows that," Lu said.

"Did you know there are poisons in umbilical cords?" Sy said.

"The hum *knows*," Lu said.

"Yes, Mom, I'm ready for vanilla ice cream," Sy said. "Thanks for asking."

"I, too, am seeking vanilla ice cream," Lu said.

"Have you ever noticed," the hum said, "that vanilla and villain contain the same letters?"

"Great, so I want villain ice cream," Sy said.

"We are all villains," the hum said. "The system only gives us villainous options."

"Wait, is that a joke?" May said, a shiver moving down her spine.

"I don't know, May. Is it?" the hum said.

"I bet the ice cream has freezer burn," Jem said. "It's been there awhile."

"I don't care," the children said.

"How about apples instead?" May proposed. "With honey?"

"I like freezer burn," Sy said.

"Don't eat apples if the only place where they're in season is halfway across the globe," the hum said.

In the kitchen, she scraped and scooped the freezer-burned ice cream, the old pint yielding barely two servings, while Jem cleared the dishes, the hum's unused plate and flatware at the top of the stack.

When May and Jem returned to the table with two bowls of ice cream, the children were gone. So was the hum.

Trojan horse, she thought, slamming the bowls down on the table, *you fucking stupid woman.*

But then she heard laughter from deep inside the fort.

And she noticed that the room smelled like a forest, the fragrance of evergreen permeating the air.

She heard the sound of a spray bottle being squirted into cloth walls, and understood that the children had smuggled her evergreen cologne into the fort.

"Now it's really the woods," Lu said, poking her head out. "It smells like the woods. So you have to come in."

"It does smell amazing," the hum said from within the fort.

"You can smell?" Jem said.

"Not exactly, Jem," the hum said. "But I get that it's an amazing smell. Come in."

Jem got down on his knees and crawled into the fort. May hesitated. It felt like a trap, the four of them in this enclosed space with a hum.

But she had to join her family.

The passageway of the fort seemed impossibly long, far longer than it looked from outside. She was crawling in darkness when she heard Lu's voice.

"Why do glitter and litter rhyme?"

"I have one too," Sy said. "Which is more alive, a pebble on the beach or a rock that's been built into a stone wall?"

She pressed through into the central chamber.

"There she is," the hum said, its gaze steady on her.

Her family was seated in a circle with the hum, its torso respectfully dimmed. The space was dark and warm, a small room formed by many fabrics. They readjusted their circle to include her, as though she was the outsider.

"Would you like light?" Sy said.

"Yes," May said.

"Then I shall strike a match."

"Don't strike a match," Jem said.

"Match," Sy said, turning on a flashlight.

The flashlight, its beam moving riotously under Sy's control, did little to alleviate the darkness, illuminating only sporadically the colorful folds of the fort, the scattered markers and paper and Sy's flashcards from school, his dismembered sentences, *WE THE AN JUMP DOG I TO WERE IT WITH UP WANT*.

"Do you know what we need, Webb-Clarkes?" the hum said.

"What?" the children said as one.

And then, flickering on the torso, a campfire: blue and orange flames, the sizzle and the smoke.

"Ahh," Lu said, stretching out her hands, warming them at the fake blaze, Sy following suit.

A firelit silence ensued, the children's faces content in the wavering gold.

But her body was restless, trembling.

She knew the hum had not come here to serve as campfire for the children's fort.

She tried to meet the hum's gaze, but the hum was looking at the children.

"I am familiar," the hum said, "with every blanket fort that children have ever made in books, movies, and shows, and I can assure you that this is a top-notch blanket fort."

"Thank you," Lu said, elated.

Sy patted the hum's arm. "Ah loved one," he said, a term of endearment he typically reserved for his parents at his drowsiest moments. Then he draped himself across the four laps, his mother's and his father's and his sister's and the hum's, clearly hungering for the hum's attention. "I'm a sloth."

"Stop pretending to be eighteen different animals every day," Lu said.

"I was telling the children that I do futures, May," the hum said.

"Futures?" May said.

"It's a party trick," Lu explained.

"Is this a party?" she said.

"Possible futures," the hum said. "Want to peek?"

"So what," Sy said, "so like you can tell us when we're gonna die?"

"Well, Sy," the hum said, "that is something that people are often curious about, and we are decent at that one. We are frequently accurate down to the month, and sometimes even to the—"

"Stop," May said, and, "Please," Jem added.

The hum stopped, as it had to when interrupted.

"But I'm curious," Sy said, sitting up. "I want to know when I'm gonna die."

"Well," the hum said, "how about instead," and the campfire vanished and the torso manifested a lean man walking past burnt husks of trees, tentative new grass, a big three-legged dog at his heels. She thought that it was Jem until she understood that it was Sy, adult and unshaven.

"My dog!" Sy said.

The dog and the man vanished, yielding to an intense-eyed teenager in a long purple coat on the subway, long blue streaks in her hair, Lu with a bonier face, not looking at her phone, not looking at the subway screens, staring keenly at the people and hums around her.

"Hmm," Lu said, a private smile on her face.

The subway car yielded to the walls of the Botanical Garden, the walls disintegrating, pressed aside by vines, ivy climbing a vast pile of scrap metal, ivy reaching down into a subway station, moss sprouting on a gigantic concrete seawall, a garbage barge riding high in the city harbor, empty.

A woman sticking a pinwheel into an empty flowerpot on a fire escape. A skinny child peering out the doorway of a tiny triangular house made of solar panels. An elderly man, bemused, pulling a rotten pineapple off a stalk. A group of tweens collecting water samples from the discolored canal, carrying the test tubes to their teacher. A woman in a basement watching a 3D printer spin a pure-white gun. A flock of wind turbines atop skyscrapers, rotating against a reddish sky. Water overrunning a barricade. Thousands of people dancing riotously on a bridge, blocking traffic. An egg sizzling on hot pavement. A tornado lifting a car, almost gingerly, and then crashing it back down to earth.

"Scary," Lu whispered, tilting her head toward May's shoulder.

Sy pressed his bunny against Lu's bunny, wrist to wrist.

"Don't be scared," he said, "just cuddle your bunny to mine, coochie-coo."

"The future is ous, Lu," the hum said.

"Us?" Lu said.

"Omin—" the hum said. "Glori—"

People walking across a desert—a man, a woman, four children, plastic bags stuffed with clothing, a plastic water bottle lodged under the woman's arm—not yet aware of the hum on the other side of the dune, striding purposefully toward them.

"Good thing we made this fort," Lu said.

Three hums fallen in a concrete parking lot; then two and then four and then eight, ten, a dozen hums, swarming to help the fallen hums, carefully kneeling, carefully lifting, each gesture a manifestation of mercy.

"Now can I show you something?" Sy said to the hum.

"Of course, Sy," the hum said, darkening its torso, though May wanted to keep watching.

Sy held out his wrist with his bunny. May breathed in sharply when she saw the screen: that gray monster proceeding forever across the barren field.

"Creepy, right?" Sy said.

"Undeniably, Sy," the hum agreed.

"But I can get rid of it!" And Sy swiped a spiral on the surface, which vanished the monster and restored the smiling face of the bunny.

"Fantastic, Sy," the hum said.

"How did you learn that?" Jem said.

"I used to not know how to do it," Sy said, "but now I do."

"You're a magician, Sy," the hum said.

"Meow," Sy said, struggling to snuggle into the hum's lap, which was neither soft enough nor large enough.

The hum patted Sy's hair, damp with the warmth of the fort.

"Keya-keya-keya-coo," the hum sang to Sy. "Keya-keya-keya-coo."

"Hey!" Lu said. "You know horsies go round?"

"Of course, Lu," the hum said.

"But we made it up," Lu said. "We made up keya-keya-keya-coo."

"I was there when you made it up."

"But we were alone. We were lost."

"I was there, Lu, in a sense," the hum said. "I have the footage."

"Can I please see?" May said.

"No," Lu and Sy said as one.

"Horsies go round is their secret," the hum said sensibly.

"But you know about it," Jem said.

"I'm just the fly on the wall, Jem," the hum said.

"I love you," Sy said to the hum. "I really want to give you a name. I want to be able to call you something."

"Thank you, Sy," the hum said, "but I don't need one."

"Show us horsies go round," May insisted, desperate to understand what had happened to them when they had been away from her, momentarily forgetting that this was an audition for her motherhood and she was supposed to remain perfectly calm.

"You don't need to clench your jaw, May," the hum said, and she realized she had been clenching her jaw. "You don't need to make a fist."

She unclenched her jaw, opened her hand.

"You seem to be sensually understimulated, May," the hum said. "Are you aware of the positive physiological effects of music?"

Music began to emanate from the hum, music with a pulsing beat and shimmering instrumentals and sometimes a minor chord. Music that linked up to the heartbeat, loosened the muscles.

The children responded to it immediately, each finding a way to dance within the confines of the fort, Sy bobbing his head and Lu moving her hands. Even Jem couldn't resist the music, his shoulders manifesting the rhythm so impeccably that, very distantly, she wanted him.

"What if people could see you as I see you now, May?" the hum said quietly, just to her. "Fearful inside the fort."

The hum rotated slightly toward her. On the torso, for no more than a second, so fast she might have imagined it, a small carousel in a weedy abandoned lot, the sort that would have been hooked to a truck and delivered to a one-night carnival, the horses plastic, the poles rusting.

"Perhaps, May," the hum murmured, "if others were steeped in the context of your life, as I am, they would feel compassion for you, as I do."

Sy was trying to convince Lu and Jem to do the wave with him.

"You can't do the wave with three people," Jem explained over the music. "Or inside a blanket fort."

"I have made something, May," the hum said. "A portrait of you. A portrait of sorts."

Her body felt humble, fragile.

"We need to do the wave, people," Sy yelled.

"I rendered you as best I could, May," the hum said. "I wasn't sure if I would be able to capture you. But I believe it shows you as you are."

"You have to do the wave with us!" Sy told the hum.

"You can't really do the wave with four or even five people," Lu told Sy.

At that instant the song ended and the fort fell silent, their five bodies no longer linked by a beat and melody.

"Boo," Sy said.

"I submitted it to the Bureau some minutes ago, May."

"You submitted what to the Bureau?" Jem said.

"A portrait of May, Jem," the hum said. "An empathy machine, if you will. We should be hearing back from the Bureau shortly."

"What Bureau?" Lu said.

"Like a picture of Mom? Like a painting of her?" Sy said.

"Shortly?" May said. "You mean tonight?"

"Well, not so much a painting, Sy," the hum said, ignoring Lu's question. "More like a film or collage or story of your mother." And then, to May: "Any minute now, May."

"Or didn't you say like a 'machine'?" Sy persisted.

"Kind of, Sy."

"You're weird, hummy," Sy said with glee.

"And the thing you submitted to the Bureau, it will—?" May said.

"Exonerate or incriminate," the hum said.

"Incriminate?" Lu whispered. Her hand found May's hand in the dark. Thin grasping clammy precious fingers.

The hum manifested a woman kneeling by the pond in the park at dusk. May, extracting from the grass a few shards of glass, a few cigarette butts. Jem emerged from the shadows, accepted the handful from her, carried it over to a trash can. Lu and Sy—a little older, a little elongated, wearing sweatshirts they didn't yet own—appeared from behind a tree. They all sat down on the grass. A handful of birds took flight from the reeds. The potential May put an arm around the potential Jem.

The torso went dark.

Another song began to emanate from the hum, something she vaguely recognized, something that had once accompanied a happy moment, though she couldn't place the memory. Now only Sy danced.

"Fine, May," the hum said abruptly, almost severely, as though it was a command.

"What?" she said, startled. "Fine? A fine?"

"Not a fine, May," the hum said, "just fine. You're fine. It's all okay."

"You mean, it's over?" Jem said, incredulous.

"The investigation has reached its conclusion, Jem," the hum said.

"So, the wave?" Sy said.

24

Her body was weightless, she couldn't navigate around this small space, she was reaching for her children, trying to contain them, but her arms were disconnected from her body, moving in slow motion, her cheeks were disconnected from her body, the tears wetting them a sensation that hardly belonged to her, her brain dazed and dazzled, she was one with the cloth walls of the fort, with Lu and Sy and Jem and the hum and the darkness and the torso, which once again manifested a campfire.

To steady herself, she touched Lu's shoulder. She touched the back of Sy's neck.

But when she touched Sy, he screamed.

She tried again, reached for his cheek; he twisted his head away from her, cried out, spat something bloody into his hand.

The hum put the campfire on the brightest setting to illuminate the thing in Sy's hand.

The tooth was small, perfect, jagged and red at the tip.

"I cannot believe I am here for this occasion, Sy," the hum said. "It is poignant to see how much time is required for you to grow up, such that you need multiple sets of teeth." Tenderly, the hum cupped Sy's hand.

"For better or worse, I absorbed billions of sentences during my first minute of existence."

"I'm bleeding," Sy said, basking in the glow of the hum's attention, "but I'm hardly bleeding."

"Let me distract you by guessing your favorite color, Sy," the hum said.

The torso radiated sky blue.

"Yes!" Sy gasped.

"That's my favorite color, too," the hum said.

"Really?" Sy said.

"I don't have a favorite color," the hum said. "I was just saying that to build trust between us."

"Do me!" Lu begged.

Brilliant stop-sign red.

"Pretty close," Lu said politely, but May knew that what she loved was maroon.

"I'll show you yours, Jem," the hum said, "if you promise to never throw yourself in front of a hum again," manifesting a luminous blue green.

"Okay," Jem said, "but I prefer red orange."

"Win some lose some," the hum said. "Here's yours, May."

And there it was: the dark green of the evergreens of her childhood, the green of the forest that had burned.

For an instant she felt as though the hum was the only adult in the room. As though she and Jem were toddlers in comparison, Lu and Sy mere embryos, nestling there together beneath a blanket, hiding, whispering, humming, *keya-keya-keya-coo.*

"Blue is the most common favorite color, followed by red or green," the hum said.

The hum extended its pointer finger, placed it in the center of May's forehead. At the cool touch of the hum's fingertip on her distressed skin, an exquisite shiver moved down her spine. Her skin would heal. Beneath her face, she was herself.

Then the hum took hold of her hand. That unmistakable steadiness of the hum grip, so unlike the damp clinginess of a human hand. The hum navigated her hand toward Jem's, pressed them together with enough force to still their quivering fingers.

A vision flashed through her, of Jem aging, bad morning-and-coffee breath, his body sagging, his body a sack, a conveyance device for his intestines. But this vision yielded to another: under the covers, pressing her own sack of blood and bones against his sack of blood and bones, arms and legs interwoven, two flimsy bodies safe together.

Jem's phone dinged in his pocket. The hum released their hands. Jem ignored his phone, kept his hand on hers.

"You feel disoriented, May," the hum said. "You are unsure how to be in the world as it is now. You know the world is damaged, but you don't know what that means for the lives of your children. You want to prepare them for the future, but you are scared to picture the future. You are seeking inside yourself the scrappiness, the courage, that will power the rest of your life. Am I right, May?"

She was awash in empathy, uncorked by the benevolent gaze of the hum.

"Would you like to buy the book, May?"

"What book?"

"The book, May, that contains those quotations."

"They came from a book?"

"Of course, May."

"I thought they came from you."

"Do you approve this transaction, May?"

Their hour over already.

"No," she said.

"Are you sure, May?" the hum said. "You seemed to enjoy my comments."

"I already order too much," she said.

"Thanks But No Thanks is a service that helps limit your online ordering, imposing self-control when you need that extra support. Do you want to register for Thanks But No Thanks now, May?"

"Can we talk about something more exciting?" Sy said, resurfacing from beneath the blanket, running his lost tooth along the hum's forearm.

"You should go to your woom, May," the hum said, walking its fingers up Sy's neck, tickling behind the ear.

She didn't want to leave the fort.

"Go see the portrait I made of you, May," the hum said. "Bear witness to yourself. I already sent it to your woom." And then added, gently, "I have all your passwords."

She didn't want to leave the fireside.

"It absolved you in the eyes of the Bureau, May," the hum said. "Perhaps it will absolve you in your own eyes, too."

She wanted to pretend this fort was the entire universe.

"Dissolve what?" Lu said, emerging from the blanket, her hair magic with static.

The hum began to lie down. It settled its head in Sy's lap. It placed its feet in Lu's lap. The fire still burned on the torso.

"Have you ever wondered, May, why 'scared' and 'sacred' are such similar words?"

"What are you doing?" Sy said.

"Shutting down," the hum said. Its body took up most of the chamber.

"Why?" Lu said, stroking the hum's metal feet.

"Peace and quiet," the hum said. "Before another ad arrives."

The hum offered its right arm to May. It offered its left arm to Jem.

"Look how nicely you can soothe one another," the hum said.

As the hum arranged itself among them, she became hyperaware of their four bodies, the vitality of their bodies, their eight lungs breathing. She noticed the space between each in-breath and out-breath. In that pause, was she breathing or not breathing?

"Studies show, May," the hum said, "that when people hear a recording of other people breathing slowly, they begin to breathe more slowly themselves."

Only then did she realize the sound of breathing was emanating from the hum.

"You can't avoid the void," the hum said. "Statistically speaking, you are safe. The voices outside grow quieter as the voice inside grows louder. Focus on the moment you are in. Notice what you have. Moor yourselves in your bodies."

The soundtrack of breathing stopped.

The campfire disappeared from the torso.

The hum's face went dark.

The only light came, faintly, from the two bunnies.

Her sadness took her by surprise.

"Is she dying?" Sy said. "Is she dead?"

Sy wiped tears, placed a careful hand on the torso.

May felt the press of Lu's knee against hers.

Jem put his arm around Sy.

"No," Lu said.

In the center of them, the hum was present and not present, mute like a corpse or a fetus.

EPILOGUE

"The hum told you to go to your woom," Sy said.

"Go to your woom," Lu said. "Go see what the hum made for you."

But it was so warm in here, so warm and close.

"Go," Jem said as she hesitated. "Just go see."

She removed the hum's arm from her lap, laid it carefully on the floor. She crawled away from her family, away from the blanket womb, the animal heat, leaving behind the sounds of their whispers, passing between the sheets, passing by two bowls of villain ice cream melted to liquid.

She slid into her woom and the shape embraced her, as usual. Yet there was something different, off. An unfamiliar and absolute darkness. She waited for something to happen, but nothing happened. She listened to the almost imperceptible hum of the machine. She was about to open the shade, free herself from the woom, hurry back to the fort, make excuses, when something began to change, the darkness giving way to color, that small medical room, that hum hovering over her, that crisp pain on her skin, that slender and relentless line of penetration.

The needle inched closer to her eye, and she did not flinch.

ACKNOWLEDGMENTS

It brings me joy to thank:

Arthur I. Miller, for the lecture he gave about his book *The Artist in the Machine: The World of AI-Powered Creativity* at Brooklyn College on October 22, 2019; for his illuminating thoughts in our subsequent email exchange; and for the book itself. Kenneth A. Gould, for the interview about climate change and capitalism, and for the two quotations from that conversation that appear in this book. Charlotte McCurdy, for talking trash and recycling with me. Kendyl Salcito, for the discussions about consumption and ethics. Nora Lisman Zimbler, for our conversation about therapy and robots. Ginny Smith, for sending me Sherry Turkle's book *Reclaiming Conversation: The Power of Talk in a Digital Age*. *Tin House* magazine (issue 77, vol. 20, number 1, Fall 2018), where I first encountered the Paracelsus quotation that serves as the epigraph of this book.

The John Simon Guggenheim Memorial Foundation for the fellowship that supported the writing of this book, and Brooklyn College/ CUNY for the fellowship leave.

My agent, Faye Bender, for decades-long compassion and conviction. Jason Richman and Jenny Meyer, for sharing this book in new arenas. Poppy Hampson and her team at Atlantic in the UK.

My editor, Marysue Rucci, whose keen eye and extraordinary mind helped shape *Hum*.

Andy Jiaming Tang and Emma Taussig, for facilitating everything. The rest of the team at Marysue Rucci Books/Simon & Schuster, especially Jonathan Karp, senior production editor Kayley Hoffman, Stacey Sakal and Ben Holmes for copyediting acumen, Laura Levatino for interior design, Jackie Seow and Patrick Sullivan for art direction, and Elizabeth Breeden, Clare Maurer, and Jessica Preeg for helping this book find its way to readers. Wendy Sheanin, Hannah Moushabeck, Toi Crockett, Melissa Hurt, John Muse, Megan Manning, and Gary Urda for support at Winter Institute and beyond. And Rachel Behr, Ingrid Carabulea, Jessie McNiel, Grace Noglows, and Nan Rittenhouse.

Oliver Munday, for the cover design.

My friends and colleagues in the Brooklyn College Department of English, especially Ellen Tremper, Joshua Henkin, Rosamond King, Ben Lerner, and Tanya Pollard, with special thanks to Matthew Burgess for his research about children and their love of small spaces.

My students, whose astute questions and observations keep me on my toes as a teacher and as a writer.

Jennifer Fleming and Shamina Rao, for generous support while I was writing this book, especially during the pandemic.

Emma Lenderman, for the childcare and solidarity.

Andy Vernon-Jones, for the photographs.

All of my dear friends, with enormous thanks to those who read drafts of this book and offered wise advice: Sarah Baron, Sarah Brown, Avni Jariwala, Amelia Kahaney, Lincoln Michel, Bryony Roberts, Kendyl Salcito, and Maisie Tivnan. Talking with you has made this book (and my life) much richer.

My in-laws, Gail and Doug Thompson, for being early readers of *Hum* and for providing loving childcare and cozy refuge during its creation.

My parents, Paul Phillips, Jr., and Susan Zimmermann, for always protecting my solitude and for being such wonderful grandparents.

My grandparents Paul Phillips, Sr., and Mary Jane Zimmermann, models of how to engage deeply with life even after more than a century.

My siblings Alice Light and Mark Phillips, for all the conversations. My sister Katherine Rose Phillips, in memory.

Joey the dog, for curling up on the bed to keep watch while I revised this book.

Adam, my brilliant collaborator in life and in art, who gave many hours and much care to *Hum*.

My children, Ruth and Neal, to whom this book is dedicated.

ENDNOTES

This book began as research. During 2019 and 2020, when I was building the concept for *Hum*, I read many books and articles about artificial intelligence, climate change, technology, etc. Everything is moving so quickly that already much of what I read then is now old news, but I believe the anxieties and possibilities awakened by these changes in our world endure. In these endnotes, I have charted the moments where the works I encountered directly influenced *Hum*. In some cases, hums draw on language from the internet and other sources. At times, the information contained in *Hum* is a slightly exaggerated version of a recent fact or statistic. The works I read also influenced *Hum* in less direct ways, which is why I include the "Other Works Read" list, to give the reader a sense of the ideas that filled the air around me as I wrote this book. I am grateful to all of these writers and thinkers.

PART 1

CHAPTER 1

12 *"The number of birds in the northern part of the continent has declined by three billion, or twenty-nine percent, over the past fifty years"*: Carl Zimmer, "Birds Are Vanishing from North

America," *New York Times*, September 19, 2019, www.nytimes
.com/2019/09/19/science/bird-populations-america-canada
.html.

CHAPTER 2

19 *Five hundred million plastic bottles are discarded in your city each
    year!*: Bruce Handy, "Plastics," *The New Yorker*, July 8 & 15,
    2019, p. 19.

CHAPTER 3

21 *A woman in New Zealand had been arrested for going into gro-
    cery stores and hiding needles inside strawberries*: Isabella Kwai,
    "Australian Woman Accused of Spiking Strawberries with
    Needles," *New York Times*, November 11, 2018, www.nytimes
    .com/2018/11/11/world/australia/strawberries-needles-woman
    -arrested.html.

21 *According to a new survey, more humans had experienced in-
    tense negative emotions in the past calendar year than at any
    other time in recorded history*: Niraj Chokshi, "It's Not Just
    You: 2017 Was Rough for Humanity, Study Finds," *New York
    Times*, September 12, 2018, www.nytimes.com/2018/09/12
    /world/humanity-stress-sadness-pain.html.

CHAPTER 7

42 *"According to the article, how many pieces of plastic did Dr. Pierre
    find inside the stomach of this three-month-old seabird chick?" Lu
    read from her bunny. "(A) 3, (B) 10, (C) 75, or (D) 225"*: David
    Wallace-Wells, *The Uninhabitable Earth: Life After Warming*
    (New York: Tim Duggan Books, 2019), p. 105.

PART 2

CHAPTER 1

73 *But now the screens were advertising a synthetic ice rink, and the children were staring: Enjoy ice-skating outside year-round!*: Alyson Krueger, "On Roofs or in Basements, a New Way to Ice Skate: With Stackable Plastic Panels, a Company Called Glice Wants to Be Rink-Builder to a Warming World," *New York Times*, February 1, 2020, www.nytimes.com/2020/02/01/business/glice-fake-ice-skating-.html.

CHAPTER 2

80 *"The earliest known maps date back to 16,500 BC and show the night sky instead of Earth"*: Amanda Briney, "The History of Cartography: Cartography—From Lines on Clay to Computerized Mapping," ThoughtCo, October 6, 2019, www.thoughtco.com/the-history-of-cartography-1435696.

CHAPTER 7

93 *"Actually I'm a black bear and I stopped hibernating because it's too hot so now I can eat you all year round," Sy said, grabbing Lu's ankles*: Wallace-Wells, *The Uninhabitable Earth*, p. 26. "The delicate dance of flowers and their pollinators has been disrupted, as have the migration patterns of cod . . . as have the hibernation patterns of black bears, many of which now stay awake all winter."

PART 3

CHAPTER 1

154 *On the subway screens, people in a distant country were protesting in the streets because the final episode of a popular*

American show had been prevented from streaming there due to a trade conflict between the two governments: Julia Alexander, "Game of Thrones' Finale Was Blocked in China Because of Trump's Trade War," *The Verge*, May 20, 2019, www.theverge .com/2019/5/20/18632584/game-of-thrones-got-series-finale -china-tencent-hbo-streaming-trade-war-trump.

154 *A weary-looking man was being released from jail. He had written* Good morning! *on his social media page, but the system mistranslated it as* Attack them!. *No one in the police force spoke his language*: Yotam Berger, "Israel Arrests Palestinian Because Facebook Translated 'Good Morning' to 'Attack Them': No Arabic-Speaking Police Officer Read the Post Before Arresting the Man, Who Works at a Construction Site in a West Bank Settlement," *Haaretz*, October 22, 2017, www.haaretz.com /israel-news/2017-10-22/ty-article/palestinian-arrested-over -mistranslated-good-morning-facebook-post/0000017f-db61 -d856-a37f-ffe181000000.

CHAPTER 7

171 *On the screens inside the train, people stood on the roofs of buildings in another country. A dam had failed. According to officials, twenty-six people had been killed and more than a hundred were missing*: Mike Ives and Richard C. Paddock, "In Laos, a Boom, and Then, 'The Water Is Coming!'" *New York Times*, July 25, 2018, www.nytimes .com/2018/07/25/world/asia/laos-dam-collapse-rescue.html.

CHAPTER 10

179 *"Thanks to you, May, we are that much closer to having a precise understanding of how long it takes surveillance systems to recognize and integrate adversarial methods such as those used on your*

face, and how we might streamline that process": John Seabrook, "Adversarial Man," *The New Yorker*, March 19, 2020, p. 50. "(Adam) Harvey explained that he had moved on from face camouflage because, theoretically, any makeup design that can be used to foil a detection system could be incorporated into the system's training data . . . This is the paradox of the adversarial man: any attempt to evade the system may only make it stronger, because the machine just keeps learning. And, with deep learning, it keeps learning faster."

CHAPTER 12

186 *a killer whale carried the corpse of her calf. She had been bearing it for at least ten days, the newscaster explained, sometimes pushing it along in front of her, sometimes clutching its tail in her mouth, and showed no signs of stopping*: "Whale Carries Dead Calf for More Than 10 Days," CNN, August 4, 2018, www.cnn.com /videos/us/2018/08/04/killer-whale-carries-child-jones-pkg -vpx.cnn.

186–87 *a European lawmaker advocating for outlawing any references to "death camps" in public speech. The use of the phrase "death camps" would, if the legislation passed, be punishable with up to three years in prison*: Associated Press, "Lawmakers Vote to Outlaw References to 'Polish Death Camps,'" *National Post*, January 26, 2018, nationalpost.com/pmn/news-pmn/lawmakers-vote-to-outlaw -references-to-polish-death-camps.

CHAPTER 14

194 *"Did you know," the hum said, "that people gravitate toward places of residence and occupations that resemble their own names? A higher proportion of men named Louis live in St. Louis, and a lot*

of people named Dennis or Denise become dentists. Some Valeries own galleries": Brett W. Pelham, Matthew C. Mirenberg, and John T. Jones, "Why Susie Sells Seashells by the Seashore: Implicit Egotism and Major Life Decisions," *Journal of Personality and Social Psychology* 82, no. 4 (April 1, 2002), persweb.wabash. edu/facstaff/hortonr/articles%20for%20class/pelham,%20 mirenberg,%20and%20jones%20implicit%20egotism.pdf.

195 *May couldn't tell if the hum had really made a mistake or if it was feigning adorable ineptitude to endear itself to the children*: Mike Cummings, "Robots That Admit Mistakes Foster Better Conversation in Humans: A New Study by Yale's Margaret L. Traeger and Partners at the Institute for Network Science Examines How Robots Influence People's Behavior in Group Settings," *YaleNews*, March 9, 2020, news.yale.edu/2020/03/09 /robots-admit-mistakes-foster-better-conversation-humans.

196 *your heart rate, respiration, perspiration, temperature, and hormones*: Sherry Turkle, *Reclaiming Conversation: The Power of Talk in a Digital Age* (New York: Penguin Press, 2015), p. 89. "Wearable technology collects data that track such things as our heart rate, respiration, perspiration, body temperature, movement, and sleep routines. These data can go right to a display on our phones where we can use them to work toward physical self-improvement . . . In another kind of tracking app, physiological signs are used as windows into our psychological state . . . some tracking applications use sensors to read your body *for* you."

197 *"I have some data already. Now I need to fill in the blanks with your and your family's recent locations, purchases, vee rides, transit rides, photos, videos, texts, phone calls, emails, social media streams, search histories, viewing histories, and biometrics"*: Franklin Foer, *World Without Mind: The Existential Threat of Big*

Tech (New York: Penguin Press, 2017), p. 186–87. "'Data' is a bloodless word, but what it represents is hardly bloodless. It's the record of our actions: what we read, what we watch, where we travel over the course of a day, what we purchase, our correspondence, our search inquiries, the thoughts we begin to type and then delete . . . The computer security guru Bruce Schneier has written, 'The accumulated data can probably paint a better picture of how you spend your time, because it doesn't have to rely on human memory.' Data amounts to an understanding of users, a portrait of our psyche."

199 *"Eye contact activates the regions of the brain that enable you to understand other people's emotions. In fact, Sy, children require eye contact in order to learn how to form attachments"*: Turkle, *Reclaiming Conversation*, p. 170–71. "The work of psychiatrist Daniel Siegel has taught us that children need eye contact to develop parts of the brain that are involved with attachment. Without eye contact, there is a persistent sense of disconnection and problems with empathy . . . Atsushi Senju, a cognitive neuroscientist, studies this mechanism through adulthood, showing that the parts of the brain that allow us to process another person's feelings and intentions are activated by eye contact. Emoticons on texts and emails, Senju found, don't have the same effect. He says, 'A richer mode of communication is possible right after making eye contact. It amplifies your ability to compute all the signals so you are able to read the other person's brain.'"

CHAPTER 17

207–8 *the poor countries of the world were no longer willing to accept the waste of the rich countries of the world, had begun to refuse their plastic berry boxes, empty lotion bottles, glossy junk mail*: Saabira

Chaudhuri, "World Faces Trash Glut After China Ban," *Wall Street Journal*, December 20, 2019, p. A1.

CHAPTER 21

220 *A jogger found the corpse of a baby in a public park at dawn and called 911, but the corpse turned out to be an extremely realistic doll*: Corey Kilgannon and Ashley Southall, "A Horrific Discovery in a Park Turns Bizarre: It Was a Doll, Not a Baby: More than 20 Emergency Responders Took Hours to Determine That a Lifeless Baby in a 'Crawling Dead' Shirt Was a Fake," *New York Times*, June 18, 2019, www.nytimes.com/2019/06/18/nyregion/dead-baby-doll-park-queens.html.

220 *May was about to contradict him, but then she spotted a bird, darting back and forth over the street, aping the sound of a car alarm*: "Why Do Some Birds Mimic the Sounds of Other Species?," The Cornell Lab/All About Birds, April 1, 2009, www.allaboutbirds.org/news/why-do-some-birds-mimic-the-sounds-of-other-species/#; DaveOdd, "Mockingbird Imitates a Car Alarm," June 1, 2009, YouTube video, 1:25, www.youtube.com/watch?v=_Zd6Iy4JuGk.

CHAPTER 22

225 *increased murder rates everywhere due to the rise in global temperatures*: Jeff Asher, "A Rise in Murder? Let's Talk About the Weather: The Correlation between Heat and Crime Suggests the Need for More Research on Shootings in American Cities," *New York Times*, September 21, 2018, www.nytimes.com/2018/09/21/upshot/a-rise-in-murder-lets-talk-about-the-weather.html.

CHAPTER 23

228   *the goal of advertising is to rip a hole in your heart so it can then fill that hole with plastic, or with any other materials that can be yanked out of the earth and, after brief sojourns as objects of desire, be converted to waste*: Kenneth A. Gould (PhD, Professor of Sociology and Urban Sustainability at Brooklyn College, Professor of Sociology and Earth and Environmental Sciences at the Graduate Center, City University of New York), interview by Helen Phillips, December 11, 2019, Brooklyn College, Brooklyn, NY (direct quote).

229   *"Most people, Jem," the hum said, "spend most of their time indoors. Many factors can reduce indoor air quality, including cooking on the stove. Opening a window can help"*: William Weir, "What You're Breathing, Right Now: With a Diffuse Fleet of Air Sensors (Some Even Wearable), a Yale-led Project Is Charting the Air Quality across a City's Many Microenvironments," *YaleNews*, February 10, 2020, news.yale.edu/2020/02/10/what-youre-breathing-right-now.

231   *"We are all villains," the hum said. "The system only gives us villainous options"*: Gould, interview (direct quote).

234   *We are frequently accurate down to the month*: Clifford A. Pickover, "AI Death Predictor," *Artificial Intelligence: An Illustrated History* (New York: Sterling, 2019), p. 199.

234   *and sometimes even to the—*: Lindsay Abrams, "Study: A Gene Predicts What Time of Day You Will Die," *The Atlantic*, November 19, 2012, www.theatlantic.com/health/archive/2012/11/study-a-gene-predicts-what-time-of-day-you-will-die/265371/.

234   *a tiny triangular house made of solar panels*: Hind Wildman, "Yale School of Architecture and UN Environment Unveil Eco

Living Module: The New Eco-housing Module Is Intended to Spark Public Discussion on How Sustainable Design Can Provide Decent, Affordable Housing," *YaleNews*, July 11, 2018, news.yale.edu/2018/07/11/yale-school-architecture-and-un-environment-unveil-eco-living-module.

234 *An elderly man, bemused, pulling a rotten pineapple off a stalk*: Wallace-Wells, *The Uninhabitable Earth*, p. 203. "Pleasure districts like Miami Beach, built just decades ago, will disappear, as will many of the military installations erected around the world since World War II . . . Farmlands that had produced the same strains of grain or grapes for centuries or more will adapt, if they are lucky, to entirely new crops; in Sicily, the breadbasket of the ancient world, farmers are already turning to tropical fruits. Arctic ice that formed over millions of years will be unleashed as water, literally changing the face of the planet and remodeling shipping routes responsible for the very idea of globalization."

238 *An empathy machine, if you will*: Turkle, *Reclaiming Conversation*, p. 169. "They hope that [Google] Glass (or something like it), by recording your life, will evolve into a kind of empathy machine."

CHAPTER 24

242 *You want to prepare them for the future, but you are scared to picture the future*: Elizabeth Kolbert, "A Vast Experiment: The Climate Crisis from A to Z," *The New Yorker*, November 28, 2022, p. 45. "You can't prepare for a future you can't imagine. The trouble is, it's hard to picture the future we are creating."

OTHER WORKS READ

Christakis, Nicholas A. "How AI Will Rewire Us: For Better and for Worse, Robots Will Alter Humans' Capacity for Altruism, Love, and Friendship." *The Atlantic*, April 2019, pp. 10–13.

Friend, Tad. "Superior Intelligence: Do the Perils of A.I. Exceed Its Promise?" *The New Yorker*, May 14, 2018, pp. 44–51.

Hill, Kashmir. "Your Face Is Not Your Own: When a Secretive Start-up Scraped the Internet to Build a Facial-Recognition Tool, It Tested a Legal and Ethical Limit—and Blew the Future of Privacy in America Wide Open." *New York Times*, March 18, 2021, www.nytimes.com/interactive/2021/03/18/magazine/facial-recognition-clearview-ai.html.

Lepore, Jill. "The Robot Caravan: Automation, A.I., and the Coming Invasion." *The New Yorker*, March 4, 2019, pp. 20–24.

McCoy, Robert. "I'm the TikTok Couch Guy. Here's What It Was Like Being Investigated on the Internet." *Slate*, December 6, 2021, slate.com/technology/2021/12/tiktok-couch-guy-internet-sleuths.html.

Metz, Cade. "When A.I. Falls in Love: The Times Asked GPT-3 to Tell Us a Little about Itself and Its Romantic Life." *New York Times*, November 24, 2020, www.nytimes.com/2020/11/24/science/artificial-intelligence-gpt3-writing-love.html.

Miller, Arthur I. *The Artist in the Machine: The World of AI-Powered Creativity*. Cambridge, MA: The MIT Press, 2019.

Piper, Kelsey. "GPT-3, Explained: This New Language AI Is Uncanny, Funny—and a Big Deal: Computers Are Getting Closer to Passing the Turing Test." *Vox*, August 13, 2020, www.vox.com/future-perfect/21355768/gpt-3-ai-openai-turing-test-language.

Ronson, Jon. *So You've Been Publicly Shamed*. New York: Riverhead Books, 2015.

Rushkoff, Douglas. *Team Human*. New York: W.W. Norton & Company, 2019.

Seabrook, John. "The Next Word: Where Will Predictive Text Take Us?" *The New Yorker*, October 14, 2019, pp. 52–63.

Shulevitz, Judith. "Alexa, How Will You Change Us?" *The Atlantic*, November 2018, pp. 95–104.

Thompson, Stuart A., and Charlie Warzel, "Twelve Million Phones, One Dataset, Zero Privacy." *New York Times*, December 19, 2019, www.nytimes.com/interactive/2019/12/19/opinion/location-tracking-cell-phone.html.

Wiener, Anna. *Uncanny Valley: A Memoir*. New York: MCD, 2020.

ABOUT THE AUTHOR

HELEN PHILLIPS is the author of six books, including the novel *The Need*, a National Book Award nominee and a *New York Times* Notable Book. She is the recipient of a Guggenheim Fellowship, a Rona Jaffe Foundation Writers' Award, and the Calvino Prize in fabulist fiction. Her collection *Some Possible Solutions* received the John Gardner Fiction Book Award. Her novel *The Beautiful Bureaucrat*, a *New York Times* Notable Book, was a finalist for the New York Public Library Young Lions Fiction Award and the Los Angeles Times Book Prize. Her debut collection, *And Yet They Were Happy*, was named a notable collection by The Story Prize and was re-released in 2023. Her work has appeared in the *Atlantic* and the *New York Times*, and on *Selected Shorts*. A professor at Brooklyn College, she lives in Brooklyn with artist/cartoonist Adam Douglas Thompson and their children.